·The Sound of Propellers·

Also by Clive King

Stig of the Dump
Ninny's Boat

·Clive King·

The
Sound of Propellers

Illustrated by David Parkins

VIKING KESTREL

VIKING KESTREL
Penguin Books Ltd, Harmondsworth, Middlesex, England
Viking Penguin Inc., 40 West 23rd Street, New York, New York 10010, U.S.A.
Penguin Books Australia Ltd, Ringwood, Victoria, Australia
Penguin Books Canada Limited, 2801 John Street, Markham, Ontario, Canada L3R 1B4
Penguin Books (N.Z.) Ltd, 182–190 Wairau Road, Auckland 10, New Zealand

First published 1986

British Library Cataloguing in Publication Data

King, Clive
The sound of propellers.
I. Title
823'.914[J]   PZ7

ISBN 0–670–81106–8

Printed in Great Britain by
Richard Clay (The Chaucer Press) Ltd,
Bungay, Suffolk

To the boys of King's School, Rochester
– who asked for it

·Contents·

Apple-pie Order

'Bombs on the railway from Madras, then a sandstorm at Aden and lifeboats washed away in the Bay of Biscay. We did our level best to get you to school in time, didn't we, Murugan?'

Miss Tuke was talking to Mr Victorian in his cosy parlour. Mr Victorian was a stout man who seemed quite kind and jolly.

'Latecomers do have difficulty settling in,' he said.

'I'm sure Murugan will be good, and we know he is clever,' said Miss Tuke. 'God bless you, Murugan!' – and she was gone, the only person I knew in England.

Boarding school! I still didn't know what it meant. A place where you slept on boards, I had always thought.

'I will show you to your dormitory,' said Mr Victorian. *Dormitory*, that was a funny word too. Didn't it mean a kind of camel? No, that was *dromedary*. Mr Victorian led me out of his warm parlour – I don't think I ever went in it again – and up the cold front staircase.

The dormitory was a long cold room with a dozen beds in it. Boys sitting up in bed, boys undressing, boys standing by their beds in fluffy dressing-gowns, one boy kneeling down saying his prayers. There was silence as we stood in the doorway.

'Boys,' said Mr Victorian, 'this is Murugan, whom we have been expecting. I have told you about him. He is six thousand miles away from home. You will have to be kind and helpful to him.'

Eleven pairs of eyes stared at me.

'That is your bed, Murugan,' said Mr Victorian. 'Between Hodgkins and Woods. Hodgkins, you will kindly look after Murugan and show him the ropes.'

Ropes? There had been ropes on the ship, but I could see none here.

Hodgkins was a round-faced, round-eyed, plump boy with dark hair.

'Yes, sir,' said Hodgkins.

I looked at my bed. It was like the others, a bony black iron thing. Each bed had a white pillow, a cold fold of white sheet, and blankets tucked in very square and tight with a rug on top. Only the rugs were different. The boys' clothes were neatly folded on chairs, their towels were neatly hung on rollers, and beside each bed was a little cupboard with a pot in it.

'See that he undresses and performs his ablutions, Hodgkins,' Mr Victorian said. 'I will come back and put the lights out in ten minutes' time.'

He walked to the door, then turned back as if he had thought of something, and spoke to the boys again.

'You will observe that Murugan's – er – epidermis is somewhat more dusky than your own. It is not his fault, and he is as clean as you are. It will not wash off.'

It was a little joke, and an obedient titter ran round

the dormitory. I was quite glad he had said it. All those beefy pink boys were going to notice my dark skin anyway.

Mr Victorian walked away and I walked uncomfortably across that shiny floor to my bed, with all those eyes on me. Night clothes had been put out for me, jacket and trousers of thick striped flannel, fluffy dressing-gown, fluffy slippers. They were all brand new and strange to me, nothing I was used to at all. Yet they were mine, because someone had sewn little labels on each of them, J. MURUGAN. I didn't even know what the J stood for. I was used to being just Murugan.

I didn't want to undress in front of all those boys, but I supposed I had to. And somebody had to say something. The boy called Hodgkins tried a friendly smile.

'Am I to wear the pajama?' I asked him.

A giggle ran round the dormitory. Had I said something funny?

'That's right,' Hodgkins said. 'Put your pyjamas on.'

'It is very cold,' I said. 'But I think one pajama will be enough.'

Every boy in the dormitory burst out laughing!

'Why do they laugh?' I asked Hodgkins.

'They're being silly,' Hodgkins said, and called out, 'Shut up, everybody!'

Woods, the boy in the other bed next to mine, took his hand away from over his mouth. He had very fair untidy hair, pale blue eyes and a pointed nose.

'You can't just have one pyjama!' he giggled.

What were they talking about, these ignorant English boys? Pajama was an Indian word for an Indian garment. Millions of people wore it.

'In India we say pajama,' I said.

'Cheek!' exclaimed a large fat boy the other side of the

dormitory. 'Telling us how to talk!' I saw I would have to be careful.

The large boy hadn't undressed yet, so I stole glances at him to see how he did it and did the same myself. Take off your grey jacket and hang it on the chairback; undo your tie and roll it up; take off your woolly jersey and lay it on the chair; take off your black shoes and put them tidily under the cupboard; slip the striped braces off your shoulders and let down your shorts –

'Mind you don't show your epidemics!' a thin-faced boy called out, and went off into a fit of laughter that made his face red and his eyes water. Mr Victorian had said *epidermis* and I knew that meant skin, but perhaps this boy didn't know what it meant.

I was standing with my long shirt-tails hanging down. I stepped out of my shorts and underpants and pulled up my pajama trousers and tied them with the white string round my waist. I pulled off my flannel shirt and then my undervest, got into my stiff sleeping-jacket and buttoned it down the front, and put on my fluffy brown dressing-gown and tied the silky cord round me in a bow. I pulled off my long woollen stockings and put my fluffy slippers on my feet.

All that, just to go to bed! I would never get used to it. Back home I wore one or two thin cotton garments.

'I'll show you the wash-place,' Hodgkins said. He took me out of the dormitory towards a room full of little washbasins. We seemed to leave a lot of excited whispering behind us.

Hodgkins found me a pigeon-hole with a flannel, a toothbrush and a tube of toothpaste in it. I watched him as he cleaned his own teeth.

'You know how to clean your teeth, don't you?' he asked, through a lot of toothpaste suds.

'I like to do so with a neem twig,' I said.

'A *what?*' he asked.

'A twig from a tree,' I said, trying to squeeze toothpaste on to the new toothbrush.

Hodgkins stared at me with round eyes.

'You clean your teeth with a dirty old stick?' he exclaimed.

'Yes, we think toothbrush is dirty – using the same one for months!'

'Well,' said Hodgkins,' I don't think you ought to tell people things like that.'

He spat into the basin, ran the tap and filled it with water, quickly washed his face and hands, then he stood on one leg and put his other foot into the water. I tried to do the same. It wasn't much of a wash. I was used to washing all over, twice a day. But I said nothing.

We went back to the dormitory together. On the way I said to Hodgkins, 'I'm afraid I shall not sleep well in that bed.'

He laughed. 'You can't sleep on the floor, can you?'

There seemed to be some sort of commotion as we got back to the dormitory, with people scuttling back to their beds. Then there was dead silence again. Behind us in the doorway was Mr Victorian.

'Let us have calm and silence!' he intoned. 'Murugan, do you wish to say your prayers?'

What, in front of all those boys?

'I do not know what prayers to say, sir,' I answered.

Mr Victorian took a large gold watch on a gold chain from his waistcoat pocket and looked at it.

'Perhaps you had better say them quietly to yourself in bed for tonight,' he said. 'Get into bed now.'

I took off my dressing-gown and slippers, climbed on to the creaking bed, and slid my feet into the cold sheets.

I stayed there, sitting on the pillow.

'Lie down, Murugan,' said Mr Victorian. 'I am going to put the lights out.'

I stayed where I was.

'Murugan,' said Mr Victorian firmly, 'you are to lie down.'

'I cannot get into this bed, Mr Victorian, sir,' I told him. I didn't know what was stopping me. There were all the other boys, stretched out in beds just like mine, some with their eyes tight shut – though I thought they were only pretending to sleep.

Mr Victorian's voice continued firmly but kindly. 'Listen, Murugan. We know you have come a long way, and that everything must seem very strange to you. We know that some people where you come from believe in disobedience. But now you are here with us you must do the same as everybody else. It is time for lights out, and we are only asking you to go to bed.'

I lay down with my body on my pillow, my knees up to my chin, and my feet and ankles under the sheet. Mr Victorian began to lose patience.

'That is not the proper way to lie in bed,' he said more sternly. 'See how good the other boys are!'

In the right-hand bed Woods was just a tuft of pale yellow hair sticking out from the sheets. In the left-hand bed Hodgkins was lying on his side, looking at me with worried eyes.

'Please, sir,' said Hodgkins. 'He said he didn't think he could ever sleep in beds like ours.'

'That will do, Hodgkins,' Mr Victorian silenced him. 'Murugan, I order you to lie down properly in that bed!'

I dearly wanted to lie down comfortably in that bed now. But however much I struggled, something seemed to be preventing me.

'I am doing my level best, Mr Victorian, sir,' was all that I could say.

Mr Victorian strode towards me and pulled down the top sheet. I don't know what he was going to do to me – but he stopped and glared around at the petrified dormitory.

'I believe this is known as an *apple-pie bed!*' he thundered. 'I shall consider the whole dormitory responsible for this foolish and unkind prank. You will all be under silence for a week. There will be no talking at any time in this dormitory!'

He walked to the door and called out, 'Matron! Be so good as to come this way!'

The nurse-person came in, clucking and fussing, with her starched apron, hard white collar and cuffs, and white cap. She swept back the blankets on my bed. I still didn't understand what had happened, but the bottom of the top sheet seemed to have got tucked up under the pillow, leaving me only a little fold to get into.

'Well, *there!*' she clucked. 'Fancy doing this to the poor boy on his first night!'

The bed was remade. Silence and darkness at last fell on that dormitory. For weeks, months it seemed, I had lived with the clatter of railway wheels or the throb of ship's engines. Now all was quiet except for the breathing of eleven bodies. I lay in my narrow tomb of icy white sheets, knowing that I would never again be warm and alive. I wasn't unhappy. There wasn't enough of me here to feel unhappy. I had left myself behind, somewhere on that six-thousand-mile journey.

My kind friends in Madras had come to see me off at the station. But where was Shanmugam, my elder brother, the only close relative I had left? I had half hoped he would turn up at the last moment and stop me going, but nobody knew where he was. I had sat for two days in that train across India. Then I had somehow expected that getting to England would be like crossing a big river. But another life had begun on that big ship at Bombay, a life of sitting down to meals with knives and forks, and games on deck with little rings of rope, and the pyramids of Egypt like the pictures in my Bible, and Malta and Gibraltar and the terrible cold storms of the Bay of Biscay. And at last there was cold, cloudy, rainy, smoky England. Miss Tuke, who had been with me all the way, was so happy to get there, but I didn't want to leave that ship. She had told me that I had learned to behave like an English gentleman on that ship – but I wasn't sure which things you did because it was a ship and which things you did because they were English.

Anyway, here I was. I wasn't sleepy, I told myself. I would never, never sleep in this cold, stiff bed. It was quiet in that room, but noises came from the outside world.

Chuff! Chuff! Chuffchuffchuffchuff! Clink clank clinketty clanketty clink . . . Somewhere a train was settling down on its sidings for the night. The train that had taken me from the docks?

Oooommm! The watery, mournful sound of a ship's siren, not far away. My ship, perhaps, setting out for its return trip of another six thousand miles – without me.

Rrrrmmmm, rrrrmmmm, rrrrmmmm . . . the propellers of a lone aeroplane were grinding their way across the top of the night. My restless mind did sums. Aeroplanes could cruise at *a hundred and fifty miles an hour!* So how long would that take me to go back those six thousand miles? Only forty hours? That couldn't be right. My home, less than two days away? It must be a dream – a dream of me, Murugan, flying back to India, in an *aeroplane* . . .

*

Clang! Clang! Clang! What was that? The bell in the mission steeple? The engine-room bell on the ship's bridge? No. Where was I? This was the dormitory, that was daylight, and the bell was the one that was going to wake me every morning in this strange new world.

My first day at boarding school had begun. But I didn't want to leave that cosy warm bed.

2

Dark Archway

A tinny alarm clock was going *click-clack, click-clack, click-clack* on Matron's mantelpiece.

'Come along now!' Matron clucked. 'If we don't buck up we're going to be late again, aren't we?'

I got that queasy feeling in my stomach again. Not because of the medicine, but the thought of being late. Being late was about the worst thing you could do at that school – a sin. I had started the term late, I was always being late, and now I'd been there a month they weren't taking any excuses.

'Pop!' The cork came out of the bottle. The bottle had glass ridges on it to measure the doses, and a handwritten label saying, 'To be taken three times a day.' Matron poured out the red sticky liquid into a spoon.

'You're not going to make a silly face, are you?' she said, holding out the spoon. I opened my mouth and she popped the medicine in. I made a silly face and stuck my tongue out. The medicine had quite a nice peppermint taste, actually — but I didn't like Matron much.

'Trot along now,' said Matron briskly. 'You've just got time to catch up with the others. Don't forget to wrap up warm.'

I hurried down the bare wooden back stairs. Down in the dark cloakroom all the hats and coats had gone except mine. I struggled into my thick black overcoat and wound my long woolly scarf round my neck, as I went towards the outside door. If I'd put my hat on it would have been easier to do my buttons up — but you never put your hat on indoors, do you? I put it on when I got out into the yard, and the icy wind blew it off again. It was made of stiff straw, yellow and black. Those hats always blew off when it was windy.

Nobody in the yard. It was later than I thought — perhaps Matron's clock had been slow. I would have to go all the way by myself, and it was getting dark. I looked at the five-shilling wrist watch Miss Tuke had given me, and it said five minutes to four. Not yet four o'clock in the afternoon, and it was getting dark already. What a country! I was getting used to being cold nearly all the time, but I couldn't get used to so much *darkness*.

I ran out into the little park they called The Vines. Running warmed me up a bit and got me past the dark clumps of shrubs quicker. Fancy calling this place The Vines! Vines were what grapes grew on, in countries where the sun shone. Nothing grew here but cold evergreens and tall trees whose bark scaled off like scabs. And there wasn't even a stray dog about, this winter evening. No people at all.

Yes, there was somebody. A man. A *gentleman*, I ought to say.

As I came round a corner he was walking ahead of me, quite slowly. He had a grey hat and a brown overcoat and gloves and a walking stick. An ordinary sort of gentleman taking an ordinary stroll through The Vines. He even paused to pluck a leafy twig from a laurel bush. But of course there were no flowers to pick, at this dead time of year.

He wants me to overtake him. I suddenly knew this, as if his thoughts had floated back to me from under that grey hat on the cold wind. I don't know why, but I didn't want him behind me. I forgot I was in a hurry, and slowed down myself. I finished buttoning up my overcoat, and then my cold fingers needed gloves on. I fumbled for them in my overcoat pockets, among the sticky toffee-papers and the broken bits of rubber and the one soggy cotton handkerchief.

The gentleman walked on ahead of me, out of The Vines and down past the Deanery. There was another funny name! Rooks nested in rookeries, pigs were kept in piggeries, cats were sent to catteries and deans lived in deaneries. And look – there was one! A flapping black cloak, a short black skirt, and thin spindly legs with lots of buttons down the sides, making for the door of the Deanery. Of course there was only one dean here. He ran the great cathedral, like the captain of a ship.

The gentleman I was following raised his hat politely to the Dean. The Dean raised his hat to the gentleman – it had little struts on it like a bridge. In a sudden panic I thought, *I must raise my hat to the Dean too.* I had one woolly glove on and I was trying to unstick toffee-papers from the other, and every now and then I had to hold my hat on in the wind. As I passed the Deanery door I raised my hat to the back of the Dean's cloak, dropped a glove, replaced my hat on my head, bent down to pick up the glove – and the wind whipped the hat off my head and sent it bowling back the way I had come. I raced desper-

ately after it and put my foot on it. It crunched a little, but
I got it on my head again. When I looked round the Dean
had disappeared, into his own front door, I supposed, and
the gentleman was gone too. I ran on quickly, and the
running and the cold air brought my cough back.

Up to my left was the great crumbling stone archway,
making a dark tunnel across the road. I looked aside to
make sure nothing was lurking in it.

Something was. A dark shape against the lamplit street
beyond. Hat, stick, overcoat. It was the gentleman – but
what was he *doing?* Brushing the cobwebs off the
archway?

Whatever he was doing, he stopped doing it and strolled
out to meet me. We met under a street-lamp. He smiled at
me nicely and spoke. His voice was – well, I thought it
was an ordinary English gentleman's voice.

'Good evening. Cold, isn't it?'

I raised my hat.

'Good evening, sir,' I replied. 'Yes. Very cold, sir.'

He passed on, and that was that. I wished I'd thought of
something cleverer to say, but what did it matter? You just
had to be polite, didn't you?

I ran on and let myself through the iron gate. This was
the bit I didn't like at all, even in daylight. People had
been buried here a long time ago, and heavy stones had
been put on them, and your feet were walking over these
stones. I could feel my cold toes curling up in my tight
shoes as I went. My feet didn't like walking over dead
people.

The wind was moaning among the dark stones of the
huge building. I came to the big wooden door. It was shut.
I was shut out in the night.

The big wooden door had a little wooden door set in it.
I tried the handle of the little one. It turned and the door

opened inwards. I stood there, not wanting to go in now. Suppose there was nobody in there, nobody alive? I couldn't go in alone.

Moaning music came from inside. That wasn't only the wind. I'd better go in. Further inside I could see lights. And there was a big black stove, its sides glowing a dim red, doing its best to warm up those masses of icy stone and dark empty spaces. I went up to it and held out my poor cold hands.

'Take your hat off!'

The sudden voice gave me a terrible jolt. For an awful moment I thought it might be the voice of God. I had done a wicked thing, walking into this place with my hat on! I snatched it off and jumped round.

A figure in long black robes was coming towards me. In one hand it held a staff with a hook on it, and in the other a rod with flaming fire on the end. The figure reached up into the darkness with the hook, pulled down a thin chain and thrust up the flaming rod.

'Pop! Pop, pop, pop.'

The gas lamps came on.

'You want to keep away from them lamps when I light them,' the verger said. 'They pop a lot.'

As he walked away he said over his shoulder, 'Don't you know you're late, lad?'

I did know. Voices came from a lighted part of the building. They called it the Lady Chapel, though it was always full of schoolboys when I went there.

*'Lord, now lettest thou thy servant depart in peace
According to thy word . . .'*

I wished I could depart in peace. But I hadn't arrived yet. I crept towards where the singing was coming from, walking on my toes and trying not to let my shoes squeak. They were all there, the big boys and the younger ones and the teachers, some of them in white cotton gowns, all on their knees now. Well, some of them were kneeling up straight, some of them kneeling bent double with their foreheads against the backs of the seats in front of them, some just slumped forwards on their chairs with their heads in their hands. Some were looking at prayer-books, some had their eyes shut, and some looked up to heaven, or at least to the shadowy ceiling of the chapel. I could see one young boy crouched in a corner by a pillar, playing cats' cradles with an elastic band in his fingers. But I couldn't clamber to my seat over all those legs and past all those bottoms. Besides, somebody might actually be talking to God and I wouldn't want to disturb them.

I lurked by the entrance of the chapel, not knowing what to do. I could see a pair of eyes glaring straight at me. It was one of the big boys, a prefect called Griffiths, and I supposed he was on duty and didn't have time to pray properly. He made an angry sign at me, but I wasn't sure what it meant so I did nothing. Then the praying came to an end and the organ music thundered for some more singing, and I slipped in quickly at the end of my row. As I squeezed through to my empty seat I got a few pinches and kicks, and boys muttered, 'Morgan's late again' and 'O'Morrigan's for it this time!' But it was all friendly enough, and at last there I was, in my place between skinny Woods and plump Hodgkins. I felt safe now in the crowd, standing up and kneeling down together, and sometimes listening to the words that were being spoken and sung.

Safe, did I say? Safe from what? I didn't know, but while I was here in this holy old building, doing the right things with everybody else, nothing bad could happen to me. The outside world couldn't get at me, and I could think about it calmly.

> '*Stir up, we beseech Thee, O Lord, the wills of Thy faithful people; that they, plenteously bringing forth the fruit of good works, may of Thee be plenteously rewarded . . .*'

The white-gowned person who was reading out the prayer didn't seem to bother much about its meaning, but alongside me 'Mouse' Woods smothered a giggle and muttered, 'Christmas pudding!' That meant nothing to me either, not at the time. But it didn't take much to set Mouse off in a fit of giggles.

I found myself reading the words carved on the old tombstone on the floor of the chapel:

SACRED TO THE MEMORY
OF ELIZABETH
WIFE OF THE LATE
LAMENTED JOHN SYLVESTER . . .

How often was Lamented John Sylvester late? And what was he late for? I wished I hadn't read that tombstone. I didn't want to think about being late. But it wasn't my fault, was it? If it hadn't been for that gentleman in The Vines . . . It was his fault. But who was going to believe that? The gentleman hadn't even done anything odd, really. Yes, he had. He'd spoken to me. People in Rochester didn't speak to strangers. Not to scruffy schoolboys like me, anyway. But he'd only said it was cold. Yes, but he didn't need to tell me that, did he? And what *had* he been doing under that archway?

The talking and the praying and the singing came to an end, and we all walked out quietly row by row. Griffiths was waiting for me by the south door.

'You were late,' he snapped. 'Come and see me in the prefects' room at break tomorrow.'

'But I had to see Matron –' I began.

'I don't wish to discuss it now. Come and see me tomorrow.' And he strode off with his walking stick. A spatter of cold rain blew in my face, and I wasn't thinking calmly any more.

'What did Griffiths say?' It was Hodgkins, winding his scarf round and round his neck.

'It's nothing to do with him, you're a junior.' That was Woods, buttoning up his overcoat.

'He says it is,' I told him. 'He's caught me being late twice already in senior school.'

'Bad luck, Mugwumps,' Woods said heartlessly. 'But he can't give you more than three whacks.'

I shivered in the icy wind as we walked out over the dead men's stones and through the iron gate. There was the dark archway ahead.

'It's not my fault,' I said. 'There was a man.'

'Are you sure it wasn't a woman?' Woods sniggered.

'A gentleman,' I said. 'Under that archway.'

'What was he doing?' Hodgkins asked.

Well, what *had* he been doing?

'Posting a letter,' I said. That was it! But my friends both laughed.

'An unlikely story,' said Woods. 'Look, come and see!'

I didn't want to go back to the dark archway, but they took me by the arms and dragged me there.

'See what I mean?' said Woods. 'No letterbox. What's the difference between a letterbox and the backside of a cow, Mugwumps?'

'I don't know,' I said impatiently. Woods was always asking silly riddles.

'Don't you?' he cackled. 'I won't ask you to post my letters, then!'

I was peering up into the dark arch.

'Look!' I said. 'There's a crack in the stones.'

'He's right,' said Hodgkins. 'Probably a bats' nest.'

'But I saw him put a letter in it,' I said.

'Come on, Mouse, we'll soon see if it's true,' Hodgkins said. 'I'll give you a bunk up.'

He leant his head and arms against the old stone wall, and made a back for Woods, who clambered up on it. He was skinny and light enough, that's why he got called Mouse, or even Minnie Mouse. But his shoes left muddy splodges on Hodgkins' overcoat. He reached up to the crack and put his hand in.

'Not a sausage!' he called down. He shoved in his whole arm and said, 'Wait a jiffy!'

'Kayvee!' I hissed. It was the alarm call we always used. Footsteps were approaching the archway. Hodgkins looked round, and Woods tumbled and slithered to the ground. But it was only big Beasley and another older boy.

'Looking for birds' nests, Minnie?' Beasley asked scornfully.

'Bats' nests,' said Woods, dusting himself down.

'What sort of bats would live there?' Beasley demanded.

'Cricket bats,' said Woods.

'Oh, *ha, ha!*' Beasley said sneeringly, and the two of them walked on.

Woods walked on too.

'Don't you want another look?' Hodgkins asked him.

'Not with you as a stepladder,' Woods answered. We walked in silence towards the Deanery.

'Besides,' said Woods. 'I've got it.'

'Got what?' I asked.

'The letter,' he said, dragging something out of his overcoat pocket. 'Only it feels more like a –'

'Let's *see!* Let's *see!*' Hodgkins and I both cried.

'Like a tobacco-pouch,' Woods said. Huddled together under a street-lamp, we looked at the packet, wrapped in yellow oilskin.

'Don't let anyone else see it,' Hodgkins said quickly. 'Mugwumps better have it. It's his excuse for being late.'

They pushed it into my hands. I didn't want it. It wasn't mine. I suddenly felt hot all over and then cold again, and my legs went weak.

'We'd better put it back,' I said feebly.

'Not likely!' said Woods.

'But it's *stealing*,' I said. 'Perhaps it's quite *normal* for that gentleman to –'

'To put his tobacco pouch into a bats' nest on a wet Sunday evening?' Hodgkins finished for me. 'I think it's a funny thing to do.'

We walked on, with other chattering groups behind and ahead of us. I didn't dare stop to open the packet.

'Perhaps it's an astignation,' Woods said.

'A what?' Hodgkins asked.

'You know, a love letter,' said Woods. 'Meet me by moonlight behind the gasworks.'

I felt even worse, thinking of that poor gentleman waiting behind the gasworks, and his lady friend hadn't even got the letter.

Somebody had overheard what Woods said, and of course it had to be Beasley, purposely loitering ahead.

'Who's been writing love letters?' Beasley demanded.

'Murugan has,' said Hodgkins. Of course this was so unlikely – me writing love letters! – that it had to be a joke. But Beasley pretended to believe it.

'That's the spirit, O'Morrigan!' he said. 'Where does she live? I'll take it round to her and save you a penny stamp.'

We came back round the corner where I'd first met the gentleman. We weren't talking because of Beasley in front of us, but I suddenly imagined the figure there, hat, coat, gloves and stick. I spoke without thinking.

'I think he's a spy.'

Beasley spoke back over his shoulder.

'Who's a spy?'

Hodgkins said, 'Someone who listens to other people's conversations, Beasley.'

'I think he's a loony,' said Woods.

'I'll give you loony!' said Beasley threateningly. We couldn't say anything sensible with stupid Beasley there, so we shut up until we got back to the boarding house.

But then the question was *what to do with the packet?* If you're a boarder you don't have many places to call your own. I had a tuck-box in the changing room, a white wooden thing with black metal corners and lock. You weren't actually allowed to keep food in it, only a few belongings, and it had a key, but other people's keys fitted it. And in the classroom I had a locker, which didn't lock. Anyway it was tea-time, so I just shoved the pouch in my inside pocket and hoped it didn't show. Of course I desperately wanted to know what was in it. But there was no place or time to look at it – and anyway, you don't open other people's things.

Matron sat at the head of our table for tea. I wanted to talk about my mystery without giving anything away. There were things I wanted to know.

So I said to Matron, 'Matron, have we got enemies?'

'Hold your bread with your left hand and use your knife with your right, Murugan dear,' said Matron. I couldn't quite get used to eating with my left hand; it's very bad manners where I come from.

'What was it you wanted to ask, Murugan?' Matron said.

'Have we got any enemies?' I repeated.

'There are lots of *foreigners* in the world, Murugan,' Matron said. 'Of course you're not a foreigner, are you?' she added hurriedly. 'You belong to the British Empire.'

That wasn't what I wanted to know.

'Are all foreigners enemies?' I asked.

'Not at all, dear,' said Matron. 'We had our Gallant Allies in the war, didn't we?'

'The War to End Wars,' Mr Victorian's voice boomed across from the other tea-table. 'Let us hope and pray that it is so. What did you wish to know, Murugan?'

'Well, sir, if a man's not an enemy, can he be a spy?'

I could see the eyes of Woods and Hodgkins, telling me not to say too much. But Mr Victorian started on a long story of how he had nearly shot some Belgians in the trenches in 1917, thinking they were Germans. I ate my bread and jam. The story didn't help.

After tea it was letter-writing time. Everyone had to sit down and write to their parents – or their 'guardians'. I didn't like that word. It made me feel even more like a prisoner. But I was used to having no parents, I didn't know where my big brother was, and Miss Tuke was my guardian, so I wrote to her.

I got a new steel nib from my pencil-box, fitted it into the metal end of my wooden penholder, put it in my mouth and sucked it. You were supposed to do this with new nibs. I stared at the open writing pad with the school crest at the top of the page, and wondered what to write. After a while I dipped the pen into the china inkwell in the desk, shook off the bit of soggy blotting paper which you always found in these inkwells, and this is what I wrote:

Dear Miss Tuke,

It is very cold here but I am wearing my woolly vest and

underpant and flannel shirt and pullover, and overcoat
and scarf and gloves when I go out. Matron is giving me
some medicine for my cough. It is not tasting too bad,
neither is the food here. I got 4 out of 10 for English Essay
but the maths test was as easy as pie.

What other interesting news could I give her? The pouch
was pressing against my chest as I wrote and I couldn't
help thinking about it. I wrote:

I saw a man in The Vines this evening

But then what could I tell her? That we pinched his tobacco
pouch? She wouldn't like that at all. So I crossed it out,
and the end of my letter looked like this:

~~I saw a man in The Vines this~~ evening Yesterday we
watched the First XV play rugger. It was very muddy and
they lost 15–6. I am looking forward to spending the
holiday in Bude with you. I hope it is warmer there.

Yours respectfully,
Murugan

Oh, well, that would have to do. And then it was bed-
time. Up in the dormitory as I knelt beside my bed I stole a
glance at the packet. I didn't open it, but through the
oilskin wrapping I could see *pictures.*
'Let's have it, Mugwumps!' Woods' voice hissed from
the next bed. 'I'll look at it under the bedclothes.'
But I shook my head and slipped the packet under my
mattress. Into the darkness that began in my cupped hands
I spoke a silent bargain:
'*Look, it wasn't my fault I was late for evening service,
was it? And I didn't really steal the packet, did I? If I
promise not to open it, and to put it back where it came
from, will You get me off the beating?*'
I'm not sure what the answer was. And I didn't sleep

well that night. Because the pictures I saw in the packet were *aeroplanes*, and I had my flying-back-to-India dream again. But this time I was pursued by an angry Dean, with great flapping bats' wings, and a flaming rod in one hand and a great hook in the other . . .

3

My Day at School

I think I'll have to explain a bit about our school. There's Junior School and Senior School and Junior Boarding House and Senior Boarding House, but if you're a bit clever for your age you can be living in Junior House and doing lessons in Senior School, where you come under the prefects.

Got it? Well, it took me weeks to get it.

Anyway, there I was, running down through The Vines from Junior House to Senior School, determined not to be late for Assembly, when I came to a sudden stop just by that clump of evergreens. The packet! What had I done with it?

I felt all my pockets. Not there! I unslung my satchel and dumped it on the path, but the packet wasn't there either. I'd left it behind, under my mattress. Anyone might find it – Matron or the maids or anybody!

I turned and ran back, up the path, across the lane, in through the door in the high brick wall, through the yard and in by the door near the cloakroom.

I stopped at the foot of the stairs. The dormitories were Out of Bounds in the daytime. You had to ask permission to go to your own bed. But I hadn't got time to ask, and I'd have to risk it. I crept up the boxy wooden stairs as quietly as I could, and across the linoleum of the landing. Nobody seemed to be about, and the beds were still unmade.

I went across the dormitory to my bed and pushed my hand under the mattress. There was the packet. I pulled it out into the daylight – the first time I'd been able to look at it alone.

' 'Ello!'

I jumped round at the voice. A large male figure was rising from behind a bed, holding a large china pot in a large hand. It was Robert the houseboy. That's what they called him, though he was a big, untidy man. He swept the junior classrooms and polished the juniors' shoes, and it seemed that he emptied their pots too. He looked at the packet in my hand and shook his head seriously.

'That's a bacca pouch. You didn't ought to be smoking bacca, not at your age.'

We all knew that Robert was a bit, well, simple. I'm afraid I snapped at him, haughtily.

'We're *allowed* to keep our written work like this.'

He shuffled off sheepishly with the pot in his hand. I don't suppose he could read or write, so how was he to know? His face sort of crumpled, and I felt rotten.

I shoved the packet into my pocket, crept down the stairs and out of the house, and ran all the way to Senior School. Out of breath and coughing, I sneaked into Assembly – last again! I got a glare from Griffiths, but the hall clock had not quite ticked up to nine o'clock, so I wasn't really late.

We had a hymn. I hadn't the breath to sing so I even thought about the words:

Above the swamps of subterfuge and shame,
The deeds, the thoughts that honour may not name,
The halting tongue that dares not tell the whole . . .

Was that me? What was subterfuge? I wasn't sure, but it sounded nasty. And as for deeds that honour may not name, what about stealing a tobacco pouch from a bat's nest? I had to keep my bargain: it had to go back – but how?

There were two things on my mind now, all the time up to morning break: how to put the packet back, and what to say to Griffiths in the Prefects' Room.

I had a quiet moment between the first two periods. The second lesson was maths, which didn't worry me, and it was the teacher who was a bit late this time. I slid the packet out of my pocket and under the lid of my desk. Those aeroplane pictures I thought I'd seen last night, they looked more like geometry figures, harmless enough. For the first time I noticed the packet wasn't sealed down in any way; the sticky oilskin held it together. Would I be very much wickeder if I opened it and had a look?

'Let's have a squint, Morgan!' It was Jilps, the boy who sat next to me, peering inquisitively through his spectacles. He put his hand under the lid of my desk and tried to snatch the packet. I certainly wasn't going to let Jilps open it! I slammed the desk-lid down on both our arms.

'Ouch, you swine, that hurt!' Jilps hissed. Well, it hurt me too. Our hands were still wrestling for the packet under the lid.

'Some people are working! Others are not!' Mr Percival, the teacher, had appeared behind us, a little round man with a bald head. Jilps pulled his hand back, without the packet, and rubbed his arm. He couldn't make a fuss; it was my desk he'd been trapped in.

But he whispered spitefully to me as the teacher got his books ready, 'In for a whacking, aren't you? Better shove that thing down your trousers!' He only said it to gloat – but perhaps it was an idea!

'And some people don't even have their books open!' came the teacher's voice. I lifted my desk-lid to get out my *Godfrey and Price Arithmetic,* and of course there was the packet again and I only half listened to the teacher's voice as he ran through a question from the book.

'*Well*, Murugan?' Mr Percival repeated the question quickly. 'A bath is provided with a tap that will fill it in five minutes, and a waste pipe that will empty it in eight minutes. In what time will the bath be filled if both are open?'

I stared back at his round little eyes as my mind ticked over.

'Thirteen and a third minutes, sir,' I said.

Mr Percival's bald head turned an angry pink.

'I did *not* ask you to make a guess and call it out, Murugan! You have not even got your exercise book ready. Kindly open it and work out the exercise correctly!'

I did so. The class was silent except for the sound of pencils on paper. But my mind was only half on the sum as I wrote it out. I had other problems to think of.

That packet – Hodgkins had said it was my excuse for being late. But wouldn't it get me into trouble? I might as well put it down my backside so the cane wouldn't hurt so much.

Mr Percival's angry voice was heard again.

'Someone has released a most unpleasant odour into this classroom! Very well, you will all have to suffer! Cummings, open all the windows! The rest of you, get on with your work!'

There were smothered giggles as the boy went round

and opened the windows, letting in blasts of cold wintry air. And in with the fresh air came something else – a sound. The sound of great engines, roaring in the distance.

I had heard boys talk about the factory down by the River Medway – 'Shorts'. Shorts were what we wore in Junior School instead of trousers, and I used to wonder why a trouser factory should make so much noise. But now I knew that the factory made aeroplanes. That ferocious roar spoke of hundreds of gallons of aircraft fuel generating hundreds of horsepower. I gazed out of the window towards the noise, but I could only see grey clouds over slate rooftops, and a seagull.

I felt the teacher's eyes on me and turned back to the pages of *Godfrey and Price*:

> *The daily rations allowed a horse are: oats 22 pounds, hay 9 pounds, straw 4 pounds. Calculate to the nearest shilling the weekly cost per 100 horses, the prices being: oats 17 shillings 6 pence per quarter of 312 pounds . . .*

I couldn't get interested in what horses ate, not while I was listening to those aeroplane engines. Wasn't there a question about how many gallons of petrol you needed to fly to India? *Fly to India . . . get away from grey skies and chill winds . . . fly over the warm rivers and the jungles, and find my big brother Shanmugam . . .*

'Bring me your exercise book, Murugan!'

The teacher's voice brought me down to earth. I took my book and walked to the front of the class. Mr Percival dipped a pen into a bottle of red ink and checked the answers I had written. A frown wrinkled his billiard-ball head as he made neat ticks all the way down the page. He looked up at me.

'If you've copied those answers from the boy next to you, you had better confess now.'

I just gaped at him. Why ever should I do a thing like that?

'Jilps!' the teacher called out. 'Bring me your work!'

Jilps came to the desk with his book. Mr Percival put it alongside mine on the desk.

'There!' he said. 'A pity you didn't copy the workings too, Murugan. Neat figures. All properly set out. Answers underlined at the bottom.'

But his wrinkles deepened as his pen hovered over the answers Jilps had written. He made neat red crosses all down the page. All wrong! I felt sorry for Jilps.

'Go and sit down, boy!'

I started smugly back to my seat, but Mr Percival called me back.

'Not you, Murugan. Stay here!'

It was Jilps who walked smugly back to his seat, while Mr Percival screwed up his face over my exercises.

'Who ever taught you to do sums like that, boy?'

'Professor Venkatasubramaniam, sir,' I told him. I'd had special lessons in Madras. It was Mr Percival's turn to gape.

And then the bell went for the beginning of morning break. My stomach turned over. I was due to report to the Prefects' Room. But Mr Percival was still puzzling over my figures.

'I can see that's a two,' he was saying. 'But here's a one with a cross like a T and a long tail. And what's happened to this seven?'

I saw what I had done. My mind had wandered while I was doing those easy sums and I'd written them down in the old Indian figures. I felt like saying we had used them in India while the English were counting on their fingers. But I didn't want to start an argument that would make me late yet again.

'Please, sir,' I said. 'I have to go to the Prefects' Room.'

'I dare say!' Mr Percival puffed. 'And I've got a cup of tea waiting in the staff room. But we've got to do something about these figures, haven't we?'

And there he was, carefully writing out the English figures and signs in my exercise book for me to copy out twenty times, while I hopped from foot to foot and looked at the clock.

At last he let me go. I was hopping for another reason now and I couldn't ignore it. I dashed to my desk, took out the packet and ran to the outside lavatory. When I'd done what I needed to do, and without really thinking, I shoved the oilskin packet down the seat of my shorts and ran to the Prefects' Room.

Griffiths was standing there looking grimly at the clock on the wall. It showed that thirteen and a third minutes of break-time had already gone by. He let me stand there, looking at the clock too, while another long half minute passed. Then he spoke, very sarcastically.

'Murugan, don't you *have* time where you come from?'

I answered without thinking.

'Plenty. But I don't have enough here.'

We had arrived five hours early for the train at Madras, and waited quite happily at the station.

'I don't think that remark is very funny or clever,' said Griffiths. 'You have had two warnings for being persistently late. I don't suppose you've got a reasonable excuse for being late on Sunday?'

I was too rushed and muddled to make out a reasonable excuse.

'There was a man – a gentleman – posting a letter in a bats' nest – I mean in the old archway – I thought he was a spy.'

Griffiths blinked and his mouth came open, but he looked at me with a bit more interest.

'Eh? I've heard some excuses, but – well, at least that's a new one. You haven't got any *evidence*, I suppose, for your story? Or any witness? And the witness would have to be *very* reliable.'

Evidence? It was down the seat of my pants and I couldn't bring it out now. *Witness?* Yes, there was one.

'Yes, Griffiths. Very reliable witness. Very reverend. The Dean.'

I had taken the prefect's breath away again. But he recovered.

'The Dean saw a spy post a letter in a bats' nest?'

'No, not actually, Griffiths. They took off their hats to each other.'

Griffiths looked at the clock again.

'I'll give you credit for an original story, Murugan. But it won't stand up, so you can bend over. Touch your toes.'

He picked up the cane. I bent over. But it *wasn't fair*. I had only told the truth.

'What's that you've shoved down your trousers? Take it out.'

And now I hadn't even got away with that trick. I stood up and pulled out the packet.

'Hand it over.'

'It's not mine, Griffiths.'

'Not yours? It was down your backside!'

I handed over the packet and he started to open it.

'But I've promised not to open it!' I protested.

'I haven't,' said Griffiths.

He was unwrapping the sticky oilskin! He was unfolding the sheet of stiff paper, big like a map! He was staring at it, his lips moving as he read. *He would have to believe the spy story now!*

39

'Huck-a-pack-flug-zoog,' Griffiths said. It sounded nonsense to me.

'A baby aeroplane sitting on a big aeroplane,' said Griffiths. 'Someone's playing a prank on you again, Murugan.' He threw the paper on to the Prefects' Room table, scattered with motoring and aircraft magazines. 'Why aren't you touching your toes?'

I bent over again miserably. Nothing was going right. The spy story was all nonsense. I saw him swing back the cane and I shut my eyes.

Knock, knock! There was somebody at the door of the Prefects' Room. The swish of the cane didn't come.

'*Come* in!' Griffiths called out crossly.

I opened my eyes and saw the door opening. The gloating face of Jilps!

'Excuse me, Griffiths, the Headmaster wants to see Murugan immediately.'

Griffiths threw the cane into the corner.

'Go on, Murugan!' he exploded. '*Go* and see the Headmaster – and see what happens to you! And don't try any silly stories on *him!*'

I couldn't believe my luck as I straightened up and made for the door. As I passed the table I took a quick look at the big sheet of paper. Little aeroplane sitting on big aeroplane – it looked ridiculous enough. That nonsense word. And lots of figures – but somehow the figures didn't look like nonsense to me. Never mind, Griffiths had said it was all a joke. It wasn't my responsibility any more.

Out in the corridor gloating Jilps asked me, 'How many did he give you?'

'None,' I told him. 'You came in the very nick of time.'

I felt quite kindly towards Jilps, but he looked disappointed.

'The Old Man can *expel* you, you know,' he said hopefully.

Now he'd given me something else to worry about. Suppose the spy story was nonsense. I still hadn't imagined the gentleman. If he wasn't a spy he had a right to put his tobacco pouch wherever he liked, and I'd stolen it. I was a thief, and thieves could be expelled, cast into outer darkness, *and there shall be weeping and gnashing of teeth*. In the gloomy corridor that led to the Headmaster's room, I saw myself cast out into even gloomier darkness, like the place where they buried the dead people outside the cathedral. And I was weeping and gnashing my teeth, with nowhere to go, as the Bible said.

I stood for an age outside the Headmaster's door before I plucked up courage to knock.

'Come in!' said a voice, and I opened the door and stood in the doorway. The silvery head of the Old Man – that's what the boys called the Headmaster – was bent over his desk, and he was covering sheets of paper with spidery handwriting. I tried to find my voice.

'I was told you wanted to see me, sir.'

The owlish spectacles looked up and the keen eyes looked into mine.

'Do I want to see you? What is your name?'

'Murugan, sir.'

'Ah yes, of course. Sit down, Murugan, won't you?'

Sit down? I felt I should be kissing his feet. I'm not joking, we still do that in my country, to people we respect a lot. And the Headmaster – well, he was like God, wasn't he? But I sat on the edge of a stuffed leather chair.

'Do you know you're quite a problem to us, Murugan?'

Here it comes, I was thinking. *About that tobacco pouch*.

'How old are you?'

The question was so unexpected that I didn't think I'd heard correctly and he had to repeat it.

'I don't know, sir,' I answered. 'I think about eleven or twelve.'

The Old Man's silvery eyebrows went up above his gold spectacle rims.

'Murugan, you are exceptionally good at mathematics, I hear. Surely you know your own age?'

I shook my head.

'You did not, perhaps, count the candles on your last birthday cake?' he asked mildly.

Candles? Cake? What was he talking about? I must have looked stupid.

'We wish to promote you to the Senior School, but we have to know your age. Perhaps it is on your baptismal certificate?'

'No, sir.' Baptism, that was when they stood you in the river and ducked you under. They hadn't done this to me yet.

The eyebrows went up again.

'I have not been baptized, sir.'

He was quite upset. He got to his feet and his hand went to the stiff white dog-collar round his neck. He paced to the window.

'But this is serious! We must have you baptized immediately.'

I looked out of the window too. The icy rain trickled down the grey slate roofs. I thought of the slate-grey, icy River Medway.

'Please, sir, may I wait until it is a little warmer?'

He turned, and allowed himself a little smile.

'We shall see that you don't catch cold. Don't worry, I shall write to your guardian. Go back to your classroom. You are a good boy.'

I walked out into the corridor. My legs felt a little weak. A lot had happened that morning, and it had ended up with the Old Man saying I was a good boy. But that just meant he didn't know how wicked I was.

And my day was only half done. The afternoon was games, and there we were in our football togs and raincoats, marching in twos up to The Alps. Not the real Alps, of course, but the junior football field was so high above the town, and so windy and cold, that we called it The Alps.

Hodgkins was walking alongside me.

'Well?' he asked quietly. 'What about the You-Know-What?' I knew what he meant. It was our first chance that day to talk about the mysterious packet.

'Griffiths confiscated it,' I answered just as quietly. 'He thinks it's rubbish.'

As we marched up the hill, down the hill to meet us marched another group of boys. Big lads, with beefy bare knees, and they scrunched along in great boots. They looked at us with contempt as they went by and seemed to want to shout rude words at us. But there were two tough-looking men in charge of them.

'Is that the Army?' I asked Hodgkins.

'Of course not! Don't you know? Those are the Borstal boys.'

'What do they do?' I wanted to know.

'You get sent to Borstal for stealing, and things like that.'

'Could you get sent there for stealing a –?' I stopped.

'A You-Know-What? Oh, stop *worrying*, Mugwumps!' Hodgkins said.

Football on The Alps. The east wind whistled over the rough ground. My mind and body were so numb with cold that I couldn't think of it as a game. A bat and a ball on a sunny, dusty cricket ground – *that* was a game. They had put me at something called Full Back, and I did my best to keep clear of the barging and shoving and the heavy, damp leather ball.

I wasn't even listening to the cries and shouts and the shrill whistle of the bored master in charge. There was something on the wind. That sound I had heard through the open classroom window, those roaring engines. From The Alps, the sound seemed to fill the whole, invisible river valley. It grew and grew, and seemed to be racing along the valley bottom, behind the trees and houses on the edge of the hill. My eyes followed my ears – and there it was! A great, grey, smooth shape climbing steadily into the grey sky, a majestic monoplane with a boat-shaped bottom, its four powerful engines each leaving a smoky trail behind it as the blur of the propellers dragged it up into the clouds. I had never seen such a monstrous thing in the skies, and yet – that outline, where had I seen it before?

The big aeroplane on the sheet of paper.

'Goal!'

'Murugan, you weren't even watching!'

I wasn't. I was flying with that flying-boat, toward the lands of warm rivers.

Soldier of the King

Boop-boop-aburp!

The sound of the burping bugle got into my dreams. I was in Bangalore and the bugles were sounding from the barracks. I was joining the army . . .

Boop-boop-aboop-boop!

I swam up to wakefulness, out of the depths of my dreams. No, I wasn't in Bangalore. The bugles sang more sweetly there. Where was I?

Not in the cosy dormitory of the Junior Boarding House. The Christmas holidays had come and gone. I'd spent them in Bude. It wasn't any warmer than Rochester, and everyone seemed over sixty, but they'd been very kind to me and fed me lots of Christmas food, and there had been a quiet little service in the old church, when they'd sprinkled me with a little warm water. I hoped it would make me less wicked – perhaps I wouldn't be late all the time now.

And now I was waking up in the Senior House. It was

all right, some of my friends had moved up too, and at least I could wear long trousers for the rest of the winter.

Beasley came in from the roof, where he'd been blowing the bugle. That's what woke us up every morning now. I had wondered what he was doing, taking the bugle to bed with him last night. He'd been warming it up. They say a cold bugle makes an awful noise. Maybe he hadn't warmed it up enough.

'Put that man on a charge, for abusing a bugle!' somebody joked from his bed at the other end of the long dormitory.

'Bloody awful row, Beasley! Seven days' band practice!'

I couldn't make out why they were talking like that. Then I remembered. I *was* joining the army today, sort of. When I'd first heard people talking about what sounded like *the core*, I'd thought of apples. Then I'd seen it written on notices, *The Corps*. I'd thought it meant a dead body, a corpse. Now I knew it was something everyone in Senior House joined. They dressed up like soldiers and marched about, and had real rifles. I didn't want to be different from everybody else, so I said I'd join. And today was Corps day. I went over to Hodgkins' bed and pulled at his blankets.

'Stodge, do we have to put on our uniforms now?' I asked. I thought he was the only one who wouldn't laugh at me.

'After lunch,' came his sleepy voice from under the bed-clothes. He was never in a hurry to wake up, yet he was never late.

It was always a rush after breakfast in the Senior House. You had to clean your own shoes, and some of us had to clean a prefect's shoes too. Guess who my prefect was. Yes, Griffiths.

He looked at the pair I had brought him.

46

'Not bad, Murugan. Not at all bad. By the way, I came across those aeroplane drawings I confiscated last term. You don't want them back, do you?'

I shook my head. I hadn't forgotten about the mysterious packet, but I wished I could.

'Junior-school nonsense, eh, Murugan? I must throw them out.'

Then we had Shoe Parade. We all had to stand in ranks like soldiers while a prefect made sure our shoes were polished and our long trousers had neat creases in them. If you didn't have a wooden trouser-press you were supposed to put your trousers under your mattress.

And then morning chapel in the cathedral. The day-boy scholar who read the lesson from the Bible on top of the brass eagle had army boots under his white gown.

'*Stand there,*' he read, '*with your feet shod with the preparation of the gospel of peace . . .*'

But I wasn't really listening. I was worrying about those aircraft drawings again. I wished Griffiths hadn't reminded me. *Junior-school nonsense* – of course it was. And it was all months ago. Nobody had said anything more about it. If it had been a joke I didn't know who was laughing. If it wasn't a joke? Well, nobody seemed to be bothering me about it.

The scholar in the white surplice marched back to his seat, his nailed boots stamping on the stone floor and on the old grave-stones. This afternoon I would be wearing my own army boots. I wished I'd been able to ask my brother Shanmugam about joining the British Army. What would he say? *Good, learn to shoot with a rifle!* or *Have nothing to do with our oppressors?*

I got through the morning's lessons somehow, and the day's lunch too. We had what we called *wooden beans*, big flat white things that tasted of sawdust. I found my mouth was too dry to swallow them. And then everybody was polishing army boots and brass buttons and cap badges.

But where was my uniform? I had tried on the scratchy khaki trousers and tunic, second-hand from someone who had left. Matron had said something about sending them to the cleaners. But where was Matron?

'Buck up, Mugwumps!' Hodgkins said, giving his cap badge a final scrub. 'If you're late for parade you'll be shot!'

At last, there was Matron with the uniform she had forgotten to give me.

'You've plenty of time to catch up with the others,' she said brightly. I'd heard those words before. The others were already putting on their peaked caps and clumping out into The Vines. And I'd never put on the whole uniform before.

'Do you want help with your puttees?' Woods asked.

'I know puttees,' I said. 'In India we say *patti*. We invented them.'

I could have bitten my tongue off, as the English say. I'd done it again! There was always trouble when I tried to teach the English anything. Woods shrugged and marched out, and I was left with eight yards of itchy serge leg-bandage, four yards for each leg, and no idea how to put them on. Each one seemed to have a right side and a wrong side, but which was which? I tried one way on one leg and the other way on the other leg. One of them had to be right.

The changing room was empty. I put on my cap. It was the smallest they'd got, but it spun round on my head, and when I turned it didn't. I hurried out into The Vines.

So this was what it felt like to be in the Army! Your feet didn't belong to you in their heavy boots, your legs were stiff in their tight bandages, you felt that all the world was looking at you in your khaki uniform. But no. The people in the park were not looking at *me*. They just saw another small soldier in a badly fitting uniform.

I clattered in my nailed boots up the path towards the clump of evergreen shrubs. In front of me was a person in a brown overcoat and a grey hat.

No! It couldn't be!

The gentleman took one glance over his shoulder at me and moved without hurrying to the small iron gate that led out of the park. He leant against it, looking thoughtfully across the narrow road at the big holm oak that grew in the corner of our playing field. Though I knew I was late again, I slowed down to give him time to go through. But he stayed there.

What should I do? I was afraid of him.

I told myself, *This isn't the dark archway on a winter night. And you're a soldier of the King!*

I marched bravely up to the gate, took off my cap politely and coughed.

'Excuse me, sir!'

He looked round and saw me standing there with my cap off. He smiled.

'I don't think soldiers raise their caps. Aren't you supposed to salute?'

I felt silly. Nobody had taught me about saluting yet. I put my cap back on my head.

He stayed leaning on the gate and casually took a cigarette-packet from his overcoat. I watched his hands as they opened the packet, took out a cigarette and put it in his mouth. There was something wrong with those hands, something that didn't go with the smart overcoat, white collar and tie. *Grubby!* Cracked skin with dirt rubbed in, black grease under broken fingernails.

But the voice was that careful, gentlemanly voice, as he held something out to me. I thought he was offering me a smoke.

'Do you collect aeroplanes?'

The question gave me quite a shock, and I think I showed it. But he was only holding out a cigarette-card. Every packet had one of these things, and most boys collected them. I could see the little picture of an aeroplane.

His green-grey eyes looked into mine as he spoke, as if the question meant something special. But his face was smiling. He had a fattish, smoothish, greyish sort of face. Nothing special about it.

Did I collect aeroplanes? I thought of those aeroplane drawings in the mysterious packet. *That was what he meant.*

I shook my head and didn't take the card. He didn't move. From the other side of the evergreen oak came military shouts. My fellow soldiers – and here I was, facing the enemy, alone!

A big, shambling figure appeared from the other side of the road and made for the gate. It was Robert the houseboy. I was rescued – yes, but I couldn't explain all this to Robert. He was slow in ordinary things.

But Robert trudged up to the gate and pushed at the other side.

''Scuse me!' Robert's manners weren't very good – lucky for me!

The gentleman had to give way, the gate opened, Robert squeezed through, I squeezed round him, and I was running across the road to the big green wooden door under the oak.

As I flung open the door I heard the command ring out. 'Fix – *bayonets!*'

And there was the platoon of young soldiers, drawn up

in line facing me, with the wintry sunshine glinting on a score of naked bayonets, each on the end of a real rifle. And behind me was the enemy. I took a deep breath.

There's the enemy, men! CHARGE!

Well, no, I didn't actually shout anything. Perhaps they wouldn't take any notice of me. Perhaps the enemy was a harmless cigarette-card collector. Anyway, when I looked round, he wasn't there.

I wasn't even very late. While the older boys were fixing bayonets a group of awkward-looking young soldiers were still standing in line under the oak tree, waiting. I tagged on to the end of the line and pretended I'd been there all the time, as Sergeant Jordan marched briskly towards them. I knew Sergeant Jordan. He was a real old soldier who taught us Physical Training and games. Perhaps I'd better tell him about the spy.

'Right, you recruits! Let's see if we can't make soldiers of you.'

I held my hand up.

'Please, Sergeant.'

'NO talking in the ranks! Nor we *don't* hold our hands up in the Army. If the enemy likes to hold both hands up, that's different!'

Some of us laughed at the joke.

'*Silence* in the ranks! And wipe those grins off your faces!'

He got us standing to attention and inspected our dress. 'Cadet Morrigan, you're *naked!* Fall out and get dressed!'

I didn't feel naked in all that itchy uniform, but when I looked down I saw that one of my puttees was trailing yards behind me. I left the ranks and another boy showed me how to put it on properly. I fell in again.

'What we're going to do this afternoon is we're going to

learn how to salute. Salutin' to the front. On the command *To the front salute* bring the right arm up level with the shoulder bring the right hand to the peak of the cap fingers straight thumb straight palm of the hand facing forwards . . .'

Oh, well, this was the Army. They even told you what to do with your thumbs. Spy-catching would come later.

After we'd done *To the front salute* and *To the right salute* and *To the left salute* and lots of *Right turn* and *Left turn* and *About turn* and *Attention* and *Stand at ease* and *Stand easy* my mind began to feel quite empty and I stopped worrying about the spy. But then Sergeant Jordan marched off and a Cadet Sergeant came swaggering over to take charge of us. It was Griffiths, with three stripes sewn on his sleeve. My mind switched on again. Griffiths would understand what I was talking about.

'Please, Griffiths, you know that gentleman I saw –'

'NO talking in the ranks!' Sergeant Griffiths barked, outraged. So I gave up and settled down to learn marching and marking time and *At the double*. My mind went blank again. Why should I worry?

'Dis-*miss!*'

What did that mean? Oh – it meant the drills were over and I had to think for myself again. It meant I had to walk back through The Vines. But I made sure I didn't do it alone. I looked around for Hodgkins and Woods – they'd been in another squad – and we walked back together. I kept peering round the clumps of shrubs, making sure that *he* wasn't there.

'What are you looking for?' Woods asked.

'*Him*,' I said. 'You know. The gentleman. The spy.'

'Oh, *no*, Mugwumps!' Hodgkins said. 'You're not starting all that again!'

'I saw him on the way to parade,' I told them. 'He

offered me a cigarette-card and asked if I collected aeroplanes.'

This sent both my friends off into hoots of laughter, which annoyed me.

'Don't you *see*?' I demanded. '*Aeroplanes*. On the paper in that packet, there were pictures of aeroplanes!'

'How do you know?' Hodgkins asked. 'You said you didn't open it.'

'I didn't,' I told him. 'But Griffiths did. And I saw those pictures.'

'You never told us,' said Woods.

I suppose I didn't. I'd been too glad to get rid of the packet, and to forget about it. But now . . . I wondered if Griffiths had destroyed those drawings. I was a soldier of the King, even if I didn't know which way to *about turn*, and if that gentleman *was* a spy . . .

Something made me say, 'Do you think there's going to be a war?'

'My Dad says we've got to fight Hitler some time,' said Woods. 'I got a letter from home today. Would you like to come home with me this weekend?'

I couldn't believe what I'd heard. Perhaps he was talking to Hodgkins. I'd forgotten that people had homes and families.

'Well, Mugwumps?' Woods asked. 'Of course if you've got something else on, never mind.'

He knew I wouldn't have something else on. But now I knew he was talking to me, I struggled to reply.

'Are you sure it is all right with your parents?' I asked.

'Of *course!*' he said. 'That's what they wrote to me about.'

'Then please tell your parents I shall be very much honoured to accept their kind invitation,' I said.

'Oh, rot!' Woods said uncomfortably. English people

don't like it if you're *too* polite. 'Tell us what was in *your* letter.'

'What letter?' I had to ask. I hardly ever got letters.

'There was one in the rack this morning,' Hodgkins said.

I hadn't looked at the rack for days, but as soon as we got in I ran to see. There it was, a yellowish-looking envelope and a stamp with the King-Emperor's head on it. An Indian stamp. Who could be writing to me from India?

I looked at the address. Was it really for me?

To Master J. Murugan, Esquire,
The Cathedral School of King Henry VIII,
City of Rochester,
County of Kent,
England.

Where had they got all that from? But it was for me all right. And I wanted to open it without anyone breathing down my neck. Of course, young gentlemen never read other people's letters – but, you know, sometimes they do.

I took it to the downstairs lavatory and locked myself in. Before I opened it I looked at the handwriting on the envelope, but it meant nothing to me. Of course in India you can pay a letter-writer to write your whole letter for you.

I sat on the closed seat and opened the envelope. This was what I saw on the single sheet of paper, in careful letter-writer's script.

To the most distinguished and reputed scholar Murugan at the Royal School in Rochester, humble and respectful greetings from his very unworthy acquaintance, Swaminathan, apothecary at Adyar. Honourable Sir, at the very outset I beg your gracious pardon for disturbance of your divine studies, in the most fervent hope that you will condescend to give aid and succour to one of your own flesh and blood. In a nutshell, I regret to inform you that your unfortunate brother Shanmugam is in durance vile. I hesitate to bring to your highly respectable ear the shocking information that the alleged crime of which he is accused is Conspiracy to Overthrow the State. We beseech you to use your undoubted influence at the very highest level to obtain his freedom. Such is my most humble prayer.

It must be another silly joke! *Distinguished and reputed scholar* – me? *Undoubted influence at the very highest level* – Murugan who blacks the prefect's shoes? Who had played this trick on me? I nearly put the paper straight down the lavatory pan.

But I took another look at the envelope. The postmark was quite clear: A D Y A R. In this school, who knew or cared about Adyar? And who knew about dear old Swaminathan who kept the shop on the corner and sold pills and medicines? And I remembered that people – especially letter-writers – did still write this sort of stuff in India. Then it *was* from old Swaminathan! What was he trying to tell me?

I had to read it three times before I understood the message. My big brother Shanmugam, in prison on a very serious charge. They could probably hang him for it. And his friends were asking *me* to do something to help him. Why me?

I was his only brother, that was why. In India you do everything to help your brother.

But what could I do, six thousand miles away?

5

Mercury-Maia

It was half term, the beginning of the long weekend holiday. Some boys had already gone off to the station, some had no homes they could go to, some of us were waiting to be picked up. I was going home with Woods! We had packed our little brown suitcases – *attaché-cases*, we called them – and we were looking out of the window at the street. Mouse was pretending not to be excited.

A big brown Rover car with a floppy top slowed down and sounded its horn loudly.

'That's us!' Mouse shouted. 'Come *on*, Mugwumps! Got your tashy-case?'

We ran out to where the Rover had stopped in the street, a yard and a half from the kerb. There was a woman at the wheel.

'Hello, Mouse darling!' his mother called.

Woods opened the door and put his case in.

'I see you've still got the same old car, Mum,' he said.

'What about introducing your friend, William?' she reproved him.

'Sorry! Mugwumps, this is my mother.' And he flapped a hand in her direction.

'*William!*' Mrs Woods scolded. It was funny, hearing her call him William. At school we never used Christian names. 'You know better than that, dear. It is usual to introduce the *gentleman* to the *lady*.'

Mouse's nose went pink with embarrassment and he tried again.

'Mother, please may I introduce Murugan? Murugan, this is my mother, Mrs Woods.'

She held out her gloved hand with a charming smile. Her hair beneath her hat had a permanent wave, and she smelt of a perfume that reminded me pleasantly of the bazaar at home.

'How do you do, Merjerum? I'm so glad you are able to come and stay with us.'

It was funny, shaking hands with a woman's glove. I hoped I would say the right thing.

'I am doing very well, thank you, Mrs Woods. It is most kind of you to invite me to your home.'

'There, William!' she turned to her son. 'See what nice manners your friend has. We are very happy to have you – er – Marjoram.' And she gave me another dazzling smile to make up for getting my name wrong.

Honk! Honk! It was an impatient van driver behind, wanting to get past.

'These drivers are so *rude!*' Mrs Woods exclaimed. 'Can't he see we're talking? You'd better get in.'

We got in. Mouse's mother crashed the engine into gear, blew her horn at a man crossing the road in front of her, and drove off.

'How's Wat, Mummy?' Mouse asked from the back seat.

'Wat's in disgrace,' came the answer. 'He found something really loathsome and rolled in it. We had to shut him up.' I wondered who on earth they could be talking about.

'Can't Bats deal with him?' Mouse asked his mother.

'I expect she will, dear. Thank you, Constable Heaver!' This last bit she called out to a policeman who seemed to be holding up all the traffic for her at a cross-roads.

'Bats is my sister,' Mouse said to me. I was grateful for some sort of explanation. I don't think he had ever mentioned his sister to me before.

'Shall I be allowed to meet her?' I asked.

'What d'you mean?'

'In India some people lock up their daughters,' I told him.

'Good idea!' Mouse laughed. 'In England they lock up their sons. What do you think boarding school's for?'

'Now, William!' his mother scolded again. 'You know you're happier at boarding school than loafing around at home.'

But what he'd said was true. We were locked up. I had spent weeks at Rochester without speaking to a female except Matron. Would I know how to talk to an English girl of my own age?

I was amazed to find how near the school the house was. The car crunched up a short gravel drive to a tall brick house. Mouse jumped out, ran round, and opened the car door for his mother. We carried our suitcases to the house. Mouse tugged at the iron bell-pull, but the door was already opening. A cheerful woman in frilly cap and apron stood on the doormat.

'Hello, Master William. Nice to be home again?'

Then she stared at me in astonishment – and I remembered I had a dark skin. I guessed I was the first person of my sort who had come to this Rochester house.

But the housemaid said politely to me, 'May I take your case, Master – er?'

'Call him Mugwumps,' said Mouse – and I was politely addressed as *Master Mugwumps* for the rest of the week-end.

As we went into the hall Mouse asked me if I wanted to wash my hands. I didn't think they were very dirty, so he left me on the ground floor and went upstairs.

'I'll be down in a tick,' he said. 'Why not go through to the conservatory and look at the view?'

I wandered through a tall room with comfortable fur-niture, and pictures on the walls. The next room had walls of glass, and it smelt of those plants with thick rough leaves, which stood around in pots. I looked at the view of the deep Medway valley, with the cold grey river at the bottom.

'Keep still or I'll drown you!' came a voice.

I froze. There were sounds of sloshing water, and I noticed little rivulets running over the tiled floor.

But perhaps the voice wasn't speaking to me. I turned. At the other end of the room was a figure, squatting on the floor. It had a lot of blond hair, like Mouse's but much longer, and a towel was knotted round its lower half. Beyond it was a sort of bath full of soap-suds and water, with something struggling in it. Could it be a baby?

The blond head turned round, and the girl's eyes looked at me, blue and round with surprise to see me there.

'Oh! Hello, I'm Bats. You must be Mugwumps. It's not your real name, is it?'

I walked closer, trying to avoid the puddles on the floor.

'I am Murugan. How do you do?' I held out my hand politely.

'I don't want your mucky paw, you filthy creature!'

I stepped back, thinking I'd done something awful. But the girl called Bats went pink right to the end of her nose, just as Mouse did at times, and burst into giggles.

'Oh, *sorry*, I was talking to the dog, not you! How do you do?' And she held out a hand, all covered with soap-suds.

We shook hands. It was nice, holding that girl's soapy hand as she smiled up at me.

'Do you like dogs?' she asked.

I looked at the hairy black creature, standing shivering in the tin bath. The girl seemed so friendly that I answered without thinking.

'We think dog is dirty.'

She turned her back on me again, tossing her head so fiercely that again I thought I had insulted her.

'Did you hear that, Wattie *dear?*' she crooned to the animal just as if it was a baby. 'He says dog is *dirty!*'

I felt terrible. I had insulted the dog. But the girl turned her face to me and I could see that she was laughing.

'We *know* dog is dirty. That is why we wash dog.'

She turned back to the dog and growled so ferociously at it that it jumped out of the bath and bolted past me through the door, across the sitting-room and out through another door.

'Wat, come *back!*' Bats screamed. 'Stop him! Catch him!' She jumped to her feet, standing in a pool of spilt water. 'Oh, he's gone into Daddy's study! I can't go in there all drippy, Daddy will be furious. *Do* you think you could go and bring him back?'

She turned her most appealing smile on me. I'd have gone into the jungle after a tiger for her. I'd *rather* have gone after a tiger. I didn't know anything about dogs.

I ventured into the study. There was a damp trail leading

across the carpet and under the desk. But it was something *on* the desk that made me stop and stare.

Plans, drawings – blueprints, I think they're called. Aeroplanes, without wheels.

Little aeroplane sitting on big aeroplane.

The shock was so great that I just stood there in that study, forgetting all about the dog. Because now I *knew* exactly what was going to happen.

Mr Woods was going to come home. He would be wearing a brown overcoat and a grey hat. His face would be fattish, smoothish, greyish. He would have black grease under his fingernails. And he would accuse me of stealing his plans from the dark archway.

What could I do? Run away from the house?

'Are you managing?' the girl's cheerful voice came from the conservatory.

Well, getting bitten by a dog was nothing to worry about now. Perhaps I'd die of – what was it, hydrophobia? It would solve my problems. I put my hand under the desk, grabbed the dog by the wet scruff of its neck, and dragged it growling back to the conservatory.

'Oh, *thank* you!' said Bats, with a flash of her blue eyes. 'He doesn't often bite. Don't look so worried.'

If she'd only known what I was worrying about!

There was a footstep behind us on the tiles. My heart missed a beat. *Mr Woods?* But no, it was his wife. She looked at the mess of water and suds.

'Oh, *Barbara!*' she scolded. 'You might have left that till after lunch. You know your father likes it on time.'

'Nearly finished, Mummy,' Bats said cheerfully, standing over the dog and rubbing it with a towel.

'Look at your frock! Run upstairs and change it immediately. And tell William to show our guest where things are.'

As the girl and I went through the sitting-room I stole a

glance at the family photographs. Which was Mr Woods? There wasn't anything that looked like *the gentleman* – but that meant nothing.

Upstairs, Mouse was lounging in his bedroom, reading an old comic.

'Do you mind if I ask what your father's job is?' I asked him.

'He's an engineer,' Mouse answered, without looking up.

Some engineers get grease under their fingernails.

'What does he look like?' I went on.

'Nothing special. You'll see when he comes home.'

Nothing special. Just what I'd said to myself that afternoon in The Vines!

There was the sound of another car drawing up on the gravel. The front door banged. A man's footsteps came up the stairs.

Should I hide under the bed? But the footsteps stopped on the floor below.

'Children!' came the voice of Mrs Woods from below. 'Lunch is ready.'

I went down those stairs as if to my death. It would have been bad enough, this first meal in a strange house, without this awful threat hanging over me. As it was, death would be welcome. There was only one thought that stopped me running out through the front door: *it was William Woods who took the plans from the dark archway*.

Barbara came down the stairs after us, looking even prettier in a fresh blue dress. That didn't comfort me much. There was no future in our friendship. Mrs Woods smiled at us as we went into the sitting-room. She was holding a little glass with a stalk to it, filled with a light brownish liquid. Was that wine? Another glass waited on a tray – for *him*.

'Now!' said Mrs Woods brightly. 'We simply must get our guest's name right. We English are terrible at foreign names, aren't we?'

'Oh yes,' I agreed with her quickly.

'Well, you don't have to tell us so,' she laughed. 'But it's true. Say it to me slowly, please.'

But I was listening to a man's footsteps coming down the stairs. I stared at the sitting-room door. It was going to open and he was going to come in – *the gentleman*. My tongue stuck in my throat and I couldn't even pronounce my own name.

The door opened and Mr Woods came in.

A thin red sunburned face, sandy hair and moustache, and a spiky nose like Mouse's. A hairy tweed jacket and baggy trousers. The hand he held out was strong, bony, but clean.

'How d'ye do, Murugan!'

He'd got my name right, first time.

So Mr Woods, the father of Mouse and Bats, wasn't *the gentleman* after all! He didn't look anything like him. I still couldn't speak – but it was blessed relief that kept me silent now.

Mr Woods turned to his son and thumped him on the shoulder so heartily that Mouse nearly toppled over.

'Hel*lo*, William, my lad! How's school?'

Mr Woods drank off his little glass of wine, rubbed his hands in front of the coal fire, and said, 'What about a spot of lunch?'

As his wife led the way to the dining-room he opened the door for her, stood in the doorway, and sniffed.

'Curry, eh?'

'Yes, dear, in honour of our guest,' said his wife.

'Hope it's hot enough for you, Murugan. I keep telling Cook her curries aren't hot enough. She won't believe me.'

A few minutes ago I felt sure that any food would choke me. But now – *curry!* I was ravenous. Mouse politely held his mother's chair as she sat down. I thought I'd better do the same for his sister. Her nose flushed pink again as I did it, and I wondered if I was being silly – but it was worth it for the smile I got. I took my own seat, spread a clean white napkin over my lap like the others, and the maid came round with the soup.

'Mulligatawny soup as well!' Mr Woods exclaimed. 'Cook's doing wonders.'

I said, 'Pepper water.'

Mouse spluttered over a mouthful of soup and choked into his napkin.

'William! Really!' his mother scolded him again. 'Have a drink of water and try and behave.'

Mouse sipped water and recovered.

'Sorry, Mummy! It's Mugwumps – he sits there saying nothing, then he suddenly says *pepper water!*'

I thought I'd better explain. 'I am also sorry, Mrs Woods. I think your husband said *milagu tannir*. In my language that is pepper water.'

'I thought mulligatawny was Irish,' Barbara said.

Mr Woods said, 'Well, now's your chance to learn a bit of – ah – what is it? Telegu? Tamil? Kannada? Mayalayam?'

I was amazed that this man knew the names of four South Indian languages.

'Tamil is my language,' I told him.

'There you are, Barbara. Tamil. But we English are rotten at learning languages, aren't we, Murugan?'

I wasn't going to get caught agreeing again. Only the English are allowed to mock the English.

'No, sir, excuse me, some boys at school are very good at Latin.'

'Latin!' Mr Woods scoffed. '*Amo, amas, amat!* All right for the Roman Empire – no earthly use in ours!'

He rested his soup spoon on his plate and leant back in his chair. 'Do you young people realize what we're trying to do at Shorts? To make it possible to stick a shilling stamp on a letter, post it in any letterbox in this country – and have it delivered within a week to any part of the British Empire. Did you know three quarters of the earth's surface is water, eh? Anywhere there's water – and the Royal Navy to look after it – our Empire Flying-boats can come down!'

I heard Mouse murmur to Bats, 'Daddy's off again!' And Mrs Woods said quietly, 'Your soup's getting cold, dear.'

But I had been listening to him. Anywhere in the Empire in a week?

'Sir,' I asked, 'will they take people too?'

'Yes, indeed,' said Mr Woods. 'You'll be able to fly to Madras in a couple of days. Cost you a hundred pounds, though!' He laughed.

I went back to my soup. When was I likely to have a hundred pounds? If I saved every bit of my shilling-a-week pocket money? A hundred pounds was two thousand shillings. Two thousand weeks was what? Thirty-eight years. Too long to wait. I was thinking of my brother Shanmugam again.

The maid served the curry. I could see that they were all looking at me to know whether I liked it. It wasn't a real hot curry, but it was a lot better than school food.

'The curry is really very delicious, Mrs Woods,' I said. Mouse said, 'It's *hot*, if you ask me.'

'Nobody did ask you,' his father said. 'Eat up! Put some warmth into you for your walk this afternoon.'

'*Walk?*' Mouse muttered and scowled.

'*Walk?*' Bats wrinkled up her nose. We all looked out of the window at the cold grey sky.

'I've got something interesting to show you on the river,' said Mr Woods.

'The Vicar's calling to see me,' said Mrs Woods. 'But a walk will do you children good.'

William and Barbara sulked over their curry. I looked at the warm coal fire in the dining-room. But – something interesting on the river? It might be a flying-boat.

'I would very much like to walk by the river, Mr Woods,' I said. Mouse and Bats glared at me as if I had stabbed them in the back. But soon after lunch, there we were, wrapped up in overcoats and scarves, walking down the cinder path to the chilly Medway. Mr Woods even had a fleecy flying-jacket and boots.

'Are you going to fly, Daddy?' Barbara asked.

'Not exactly,' he replied mysteriously. 'Would you three like to walk on towards Wouldham Marshes? You'll see me later.'

'Oh, Daddy, that's not *fair!*' Barbara flared up. 'I thought you were coming with us. I believe you're going to *work*.'

'I promised I'd show you something interesting,' he said. 'Do what I say.'

He disappeared into the gates of the big factory on the river bank. We trudged along the muddy path in grumpy silence.

'It'd better be *very* interesting,' Bats said at last.

'It's a trick to send us on a walk,' said William.

That roar of aero-engines began to fill the valley again, but we couldn't see where it was coming from. I thought of those aeroplane pictures I'd seen on Mr Woods' desk, almost exactly the same as the ones I'd seen in the Prefects' Room. They were still a mystery.

'I say, Woods,' I began. 'You know that tobacco pouch –'

'Mouse, you've been smoking!' Bats cried. 'I'll tell Dad.'

'Shut up, Bats!' her brother snapped. 'You don't know what we're talking about. We said we wouldn't tell anybody else, Mugwumps.'

I had thought it would be nice to bring Barbara in on our secret. Now I'd started a family argument. But before it got any worse, I saw that Mouse was standing frozen, his eyes popping with amazement, looking back down the river to the factory and the slipways.

'Look at that!' Mouse squeaked, his voice breaking.

I spun round. I didn't believe what my eyes saw, though I'd seen it before – but only in pictures and in my dreams. Was I dreaming again?

Little aeroplane sitting on big aeroplane!

In the distance it looked like a Meccano toy put together for a joke. How many engines? Two, four, six – eight engines, each with a spinning propeller. It came taxiing along the brimming water towards us. The big plane had the broad hull of a flying-boat, and was sending up a white bow-wave. The plane on top had long legs with floats on the ends, a seaplane. Holding them together was a criss-cross of girders, and a little human figure was hanging on to them.

Barbara shouted above the din of the engines, 'They've got names!' We could see them painted in big letters on the hulls.

'*Mercury*,' Mouse read from the top one. 'Funny name. The stuff in thermometers.'

'*Mercury?*' Barbara repeated. 'That's the god with wings on his boots.'

'*Maia*,' I read from the flying-boat. But that word only told me I must be dreaming. *Maia . . . maya?* Indian word!

It meant – I couldn't shout what it meant above the roaring engines. It meant *world of illusion, dream world.*

As it got nearer the figure on the struts waved to us.

'*Daddy!*' Barbara screamed. The figure was wearing fleecy jacket and boots, and a flying-helmet. 'Daddy, get *inside!* That's *dangerous!*'

Mr Woods couldn't have heard anything above the noise of the eight engines as they roared past us. Now we were all running flat out along the bank, trying to keep up. But we hadn't a chance. Barbara, out in front, pulled up panting and gasping.

'Stop! We'll wait here. They'll turn round – by Cuxton. They always do – all the flying-boats.'

We went out as far as we dared on to the marshy point where the river bent round. Mouse went a bit further, jumped a little tidal creek, and covered his black school shoes with mud.

Out on the river, the four engines on one side of the contraption slowed down and the others speeded up. The two tails wagged. The planes slewed round until they were facing downstream, and into the cold east wind. Barbara, her eyes blazing, kept them on the figure of her father.

'Silly man!' she fumed. I was sorry for her; it did look dangerous, what he was doing. 'I bet he wouldn't let *me* do that. It's not fair!' she went on. No, she wasn't worried – she just wanted to do it herself!

'D'you think they're going to take off?' Barbara shouted to William, further out on the point.

'What?' he shouted back over the engine noise.

'Are they going to *fly?*' she shouted again.

'*That*'ll never fly,' we heard William's voice come back.

But all the engines speeded up and the thing moved again, downstream, upwind. A beautiful wave of spray rose from the curved bows of Maia as they moved faster and faster through the water. The spray rose higher and higher as it passed us again – and then the bow-wave fell away again. But the engines' roar was just as loud and the planes were moving just as fast. Maia's hull was rising in the water – there was no spray, she was clear of the water! The two planes were airborne together, and there was Barbara's father, still clinging to the struts between them!

I could hear William, cheering with wild excitement out on the point. But Barbara had covered her eyes with her hands. She can't have seen that Maia's hull was smoothly dipping down towards the water again, the spray was rising, the whole thing was slowing down.

I touched her arm gently. 'You may look now. They are no longer flying.'

She took her hands away from her face, then broke into a headlong run down the river path without saying a word. I ran after her, and I could hear William shouting behind us, 'Wait for me!' Ahead, we could see Mercury-Maia taxiing towards the factory slipways. William put on a spurt and caught up with us, and we ran all the way back to the factory. As we slowed down, Barbara spoke again, between deep breaths.

'Going to give – that father of mine – a piece of my mind!'

She marched up to the gate-keeper in his little hut.

'I insist on seeing Mr Woods!' she puffed.

'That's okay, miss,' the man grinned. 'You're to go straight in, he said.'

A man in overalls showed us the way. I had expected a noisy factory, but everything was quiet in that great hangar. It was a bit like going into the cathedral when it was empty, and we spoke in low voices. Great silent shapes of metal loomed over us, huge flying-boats in the making.

In another part were smaller planes, and a very strong smell.

'Peardrops,' I said. It was just like the boiled sweets we got at the tuckshop.

'Dope,' said the silent man in overalls. I thought I had said something silly and he had said something rude – but afterwards I learned it was something they put on aeroplane wings.

Now we could see out through the great sliding doors that opened on the river. A motorboat was towing Mercury-Maia towards the slipway. Another one was coming alongside the jetty with three men in it. In the water, men in floppy black wading-suits were holding the ends of mooring ropes.

As her father came ashore, Barbara ran along the jetty, gave him a hug, then immediately began to scold him.

'*Daddy*, you and your *something interesting!* What do you mean by going up in the air like that? I'm sure you're not *supposed* to!'

'I wasn't supposed to,' her father grinned. 'It was going to be a taxiing trial, but it was fun while it lasted. Don't tell Mum, will you?'

There was a laugh from the younger of the two other men – of course Mercury-Maia must have had two pilots.

'We'll log you exactly eight seconds' flying time, Woods.'

The older pilot looked more serious.

'I can only repeat that I'm most terribly sorry. I just can't make out how it happened. We *should* have been taxiing, with the airspeed indicator reading as it did.'

And at that moment one of the men in the water turned his face towards us. Nothing very special about that face: fattish, smoothish, greyish, *smiling*. In his cold, bare hands he held the mooring rope, black with greasy Medway mud . . .

The gentleman!
Did I say that out loud, or didn't I?
'Come in out of the cold,' said Mr Woods.

6

Gremlins

We came in from the cold, to the warm boardroom of the factory. A blazing coal fire, a picture of the King and Queen over the mantelpiece, framed photographs of aeroplanes on the walls. Someone brought tea for the men and sweet biscuits for us. Mr Woods gathered us, Barbara, William and me, round a polished table with a big globe of the world on it.

Mouse groaned to himself, 'Jography lesson!' as if he'd heard it all before. But I needed to learn all I could. And how much should I *tell*? Wasn't this the time to tell everything, about the packet, the plans, and the *gentleman*?

Mr Woods spun the globe. 'You know all the red bits are British Empire. We built it all up by sea, didn't we?'

'On the blue bits,' Barbara said.

'Quite right,' said her father, not sure whether she was being cheeky. 'Now the job's to keep it all together, by air. But we might as well use the blue bits to come down on, eh?'

'There is very much water on the globe,' I said. I'd never seen a globe in India.

'Isn't there?' Mr Woods agreed, spinning the globe again. 'Now you see the difficulty in getting to Canada, don't you?'

I didn't. I wasn't interested in getting to Canada. I wanted to get to India.

'Sir, there is plenty of water there,' I said, for something to say.

'Too much,' said Mr Woods. 'And no red bits between here and there. An aircraft the size of Mercury could just about fly the distance, carrying a heavy load of mail and all its own fuel. Just one snag, though – it couldn't get off the ground, or off the water. So what do we need?'

'The *Queen Mary*,' Mouse muttered. His father ignored him.

'We need something to boost the heavy-laden plane into the air. And the answer's Mercury-Maia, the composite aircraft. Maia gives Mercury a piggy-back into the air. We separate them, and Mercury flies on alone. What do you think of it?'

'Where did you get those funny names from, Daddy?' Barbara asked.

'I checked up with William's Headmaster. He's a classics man. Mercury is the winged messenger of the gods and Maia was his mother. All in the family, see?'

'I see,' said Barbara. 'But, Daddy, do you *have* to stand up there and hold them together? *I* think the whole thing's crazy!'

'Well, I'm afraid you're not the only one, Bats,' her father smiled. He turned to the pilots. 'But once these trials are over, we'll show them, won't we, chaps?'

'I'm sure you've done your sums right, Woods,' said the

older pilot. 'But why do these little things keep going wrong?'

For some reason I thought of the smile on the face of the man in the bat-like wading suit. I opened my mouth to speak, but the young pilot spoke first.

'Gremlins.'

We all looked at him. Nobody seemed to understand the word.

'I beg your pardon, Harold?' the older pilot queried.

'Gremlins,' Harold repeated.

'And what are they when they're at home?' Mr Woods asked, as mystified as the rest of us.

'They're at home in any aircraft,' Harold said airily. 'They live behind the instrument panels, drink high-octane cocktails and hydraulic fluid, and eat insulation. They go for rides on the gyro compass and sing songs to the moon over the radio.'

There was a bit of a silence in the posh boardroom.

'Are you sure you're all right, Harold, old boy?' the senior pilot asked. 'Not feeling the strain from all these tests? And what have you got in that teacup?'

'Tea,' said Harold. 'Probably from India, where I first heard of gremlins.'

Then they all looked at me. Mouse exploded with laughter and chocolate biscuit.

'*That is Indian word,*' he spluttered, and choked. Bats thumped him on the back.

I shook my head. 'I do not know any such word. They are perhaps *rakhshasas* – demons?'

'Gremlins sound much nicer,' Barbara said. 'I'm going to believe in them.'

'Thank you, Barbara,' said Harold. 'At least I'm not alone here.'

But he went on looking keenly at me.

74

'You were going to say something just then? And what was that you said out on the jetty? It sounded a bit like *the gremlin.*'

I felt very uncomfortable with everyone's eyes on me. But it was my chance to speak.

'Did I say something aloud, sir? I must have said *the gentleman.* I thought I recognized one of the men in the water.'

There was another silence. Mr Woods broke it.

'We've got a first-rate team working on the composite aircraft. Fine chaps, and they all muck in on mooring jobs. But they don't ask to be called gentlemen. Perhaps you'd like to explain.'

I knew I had to tell the whole story now. I glanced at Mouse. He looked anxious, but he didn't seem to want me to stop.

'Sir, it started last term on a Sunday evening. I was late for chapel, and I met this gentleman in The Vines, and he went into the dark archway near the cathedral and . . .'

Somehow I felt that they weren't listening. The pilots poured themselves more tea and the older one passed a silver cigarette case to Harold. Mr Woods began stuffing and lighting a pipe. His tobacco pouch was made of yellow see-through oilskin. I went on.

'. . . so when we got out of chapel Mouse got up on Stodge's back and pulled out a tobacco pouch – just like yours, sir.'

Mr Woods barked sternly through clouds of tobacco smoke.

'William, have you been smoking?'

'No, sir,' I said hastily. 'There was no tobacco in it, only papers. Hodgkins said I'd better keep it, it was my excuse for being late. But when I reported to the Prefects' Room next day I –'

I broke off, and looked across at Barbara. Would she think it very rude, what I was going to say?

'He stuffed it down the seat of his pants,' Mouse said crudely – and Bats went off into peals of laughter.

Harold guffawed. 'Same old trick! It never worked – not for me, anyway.'

I had to go on. 'But Griffiths saw it, he's the prefect. And he opened it, and I saw what was in it – pictures of a seaplane on top of a flying-boat.'

'But you never even told me that, Mugwumps!' Mouse exclaimed. Hadn't I? I suppose I'd just wanted to forget about it.

The men were listening now. Mr Woods took his pipe out of his mouth and leaned forward.

'How long ago was this, Murugan?'

'Last term, sir. About three months ago.'

'Can you describe exactly what you saw on that paper?'

I hesitated. 'Sir – it was exactly like what I saw on the desk in your study today, but a different language. I – I went in after the dog,' I explained.

'Wat was being naughty, Daddy,' Barbara came to my rescue. 'He ran into your study, all wet, and Murugan was very kind and dragged him out.'

Mr Woods breathed in a big mouthful of pipe tobacco and puffed it slowly out.

'So you're all in this – and the dog!' he exclaimed. 'But this – this *gentleman*, you only saw him in the dark?'

I told him about the second meeting, before Corps parade. I think he was a bit impressed that I was a cadet. The three men looked at each other.

'What do you think, gentlemen?' Mr Woods asked.

'There may be something fishy going on,' said the senior pilot. 'But with all respect to our young friend here, we've only his word for it. What happened to those papers? Can't we see them?'

I had to admit that Griffiths had probably thrown them out, and I began to wish I hadn't spoken. But Mr Woods was moving towards the telephone in the boardroom.

'What's the school's telephone number?' he asked.

Neither Mouse nor I knew, of course. Boarders don't use the telephone.

'Oh, Dad, you can't phone the *school*,' Mouse retorted. 'You'll probably get the Old Man!'

I knew what he meant. There might be international espionage and valuable aircraft developments involved, but you didn't bother the Headmaster about little things like that.

But Mr Woods was talking to various operators. At last a man's voice came through.

'Who's that speaking?' Mr Woods barked. 'Oh, Canon Williams, good afternoon, it's Woods of Shorts here.'

It *was* the Old Man. Would he know who Woods of Shorts was?

'No, nothing about my offspring, I'm glad to say, Canon Williams. I hate to disturb you on a weekend, but would it be possible to speak to a prefect called Griffiths? I know it's half term, but some of the boys stay behind, don't they?'

Mouse was clutching his mouth with horror. Mr Woods never asked to speak to his own son on the phone, it wasn't allowed – and here he was demanding to speak to a prefect he didn't even know! It took some time. The Old Man didn't sound at all pleased. There was a silence.

Still holding the receiver, Mr Woods turned to me.

'Let's make sure who we think we're talking about. Can you describe this *gentleman* to me?'

It's difficult to describe a face that isn't very special, but I tried.

Harold said thoughtfully, 'I've heard the men calling one of the fitters The Toff. There was some joke about him dressing up posh. His name's Webber. The description fits.'

'Webber?' Mr Woods pondered, still holding the silent telephone. 'A decent sort of chap. Well-spoken, and a skilled fitter. We've had him on fitting and checking flight instruments – my God!'

He suddenly slapped himself on the thigh and pulled a long face.

The senior pilot looked at him and said one strange word.

'*Sabotage?*'

'I can't believe it,' said Mr Woods.

'But if anyone wanted to wreck our trials, that would be the key job?' asked the pilot.

Mr Woods nodded. A voice came on the other end of the telephone. It didn't have far to travel and I could tell it belonged to Griffiths. Mr Woods replied in a hearty voice.

'Ah, Griffiths? Woods of Shorts here. You don't know me, but I've seen you on the cricket field, I think. Splendid fifty you made at the Commemoration Match! . . . Not at all. Er, I say, old boy, you don't just happen to have any of our aircraft plans in your possession, do you?'

There was quite a long silence at the other end of the phone. I enjoyed the thought that Griffiths must be feeling very uncomfortable. He spluttered something in reply but I didn't hear the words. Mr Woods went on.

'That's it, confiscated from a boy called Murugan.' He nodded across the room to the rest of us. 'No, no, I assure you I'm not blaming you in the least. Lots of other people have thought it was rubbish. Have you still got it? . . . You have? Grand! Look, can you hang on there while I get a car to collect it? . . . What? . . . You'll bring it round? On your bicycle? Splendid! Most kind of you! I'll tell the gatekeeper to let you in.'

He hung up the receiver and walked over to the fire-place.

'The evidence is on the way. On a bicycle. It shouldn't take long. Meanwhile . . .?'

I was feeling a lot better – and even looking forward to seeing Griffiths. What had he said? *Haven't got time for silly games. Junior-school nonsense.* Who was going to look silly now?

I broke the waiting silence.

'Please, what is *sabotage?*'

The senior pilot smiled a little. 'French word. The workers used to throw wooden shoes in the machinery. To clog it up, I suppose.'

'The *gentleman* wore leather shoes,' I said. At least I made them laugh.

'Daddy, have you really got a spy?' Barbara asked, bouncing up and down in her chair.

'I'm still hoping it's all childish nonsense,' her father said gruffly.

'And gremlins?' she persisted.

'Well, we can't take any chances,' he had to say.

'Murugan says he recognized the man in the water, Daddy,' she went on. 'Can't we go and *see?*'

'The girl's got a point there, Woods,' said the pilot. 'Can't we take the boy to identify him?'

I didn't feel too happy about that. I hoped it *wasn't* all childish nonsense, because then *I* would look silly. But I didn't want to confront that man.

'Please,' I said, 'I would not like him to see that I had seen him, if he is the man I saw.'

'Er – I see,' said Mr Woods. 'But I think we could arrange that. Come on, Parker!' he said to the senior pilot. 'We three will go and spy on the spy, if that's what he is.'

'Oh, Daddy, it was my idea,' Barbara protested. 'Can't I come?'

'Can't *I*, Dad?' Mouse joined in. But they both had to stay in the room with Harold.

Mr Woods, the pilot Parker and I walked along cold corridors and down to the factory. We went into a chilly, dusty storeroom with miles of shelves. It had a hatchway and a little dirty window looking out into the main hangar, where there was plenty of light. We did not put the lights on in the storeroom.

'The men will have to pass in front of that window as they come in from the slipway,' murmured Mr Woods. 'They won't see us in here, but we'll see them.'

They gave me a tall stool to sit on, to one side of the dusty window. We settled down to wait.

'How do you like being a counter-spy?' Parker murmured.

I didn't. There I was, shivering in that dark store with two large Englishmen who smelt of tobacco smoke. Who was I spying on? Some honest British workman, that I might be getting into serious trouble? Or even some courageous foreigner, doing his best for his country? He might be an enemy of the British Empire – but then so was my own brother! If only there was some way that all this could help Shanmugam, but I didn't see how it could. All these thoughts passed through my mind as we waited, listening to the storeroom clock. I had pretty well decided that I wasn't going to identify anyone, when the men started to come in from the slipway.

They passed the other side of the window, under the strong lights of the hangar, laughing and joking, glad their shift was over. Not one face that looked like the *gentleman*. Had I imagined that face on the man in the water?

'Well?' I heard Mr Woods' whispered question. I shook my head in the gloom.

One last worker trailed in from outside, some way behind the others. In his bat-like wading-suit, he passed close up to the window, turned – and there was the face looking straight in at me! It wasn't smiling.

I shrank back away from the window, against Mr Woods' rough tweed jacket. Surely I'd been seen?

The handle of the door by the window was turning. He was trying to get in!

I clutched Mr Woods' tweedy arm and hissed, 'Don't let him in!'

It must have been locked, that door. The handle stopped rattling; the bat-figure passed on after the others.

'Let's go,' murmured Mr Woods. He let us out of the door at the other end of the storeroom, and locked it behind him. He was holding my arm as we walked back along that corridor, because I was shaking all over.

'It's all right, Murugan,' he said. 'He can't have seen you.'

'It is just that I am a little c-c-cold, sir,' I managed to say.

'Of course.' He turned to Parker. 'Pretty conclusive, I think, Parker. This lad's had quite a shock. And that man had no right to enter the storeroom.'

And then there was the sound of running feet in the corridor, the springy stride of someone in light rubber-soled shoes. Round the corner came the runner, in shorts, sweater and school scarf. It was Griffiths.

He halted in front of us and stood smartly to attention. Then he saw me, and blinked.

'I'm looking for Mr Woods, sir,' said Griffiths.

'You must be Griffiths,' said Mr Woods. 'Have you got the plans?'

Out of breath, Griffiths nodded and reached inside his sweater. He pulled out the tobacco pouch, took a smart pace forward, and held it out to Mr Woods. I think he wanted to salute, but he didn't have a soldier's cap on.

'Come inside, come inside!' said Mr Woods, taking the packet. We all went into the warm boardroom, and I soon stopped shaking.

Griffiths blinked again when he saw Mouse there, and Barbara. She looked at his bare knees, and put her hand to her mouth to hide a fit of giggles.

'Good of you to come, Griffiths,' said Mr Wood. 'Did I interrupt a game of some sort?'

'Hard game of fives, sir,' said Griffiths. He was still panting. 'Found my bike had a puncture. Ran all the way.'

'Jolly good show!' said Harold.

Mr Woods was taking the paper out of the pouch and unfolding it on the table. 'Take a look at this, gentlemen,' he said to the pilots. They all bent over it.

'*Hookerpackfloogzoig.*' Parker pronounced the monstrous word carefully – and of course Mouse joined Bats in a wilder attack of giggles, the sort you get when everyone's being terribly serious.

'What a word, eh!' Harold commented.

'You see what I mean, sir?' Griffiths said eagerly. 'How can you take a thing like that seriously?'

'A perfectly serious German word for composite aircraft,' Parker said.

'And a very competent free-hand copy of our blueprints,' said Mr Woods. 'The person who copied out the formulae knew what he was doing, too.'

'But what does it all *mean*, Daddy?' Barbara asked impatiently.

Mr Woods pulled his long face.

'It may mean something that little girls must keep quiet about. And that goes for everyone else in this room, of course.'

'Yes, Daddy, but *what* mustn't we talk about? Lots of people must have seen you this afternoon, on the river.'

'All right. I'll tell you what I think, and then you must shut up about it. Someone has gone to the trouble of copying our most important plan. Someone has made notes on it in German. Someone hid it in the old archway for someone else to collect. You, William, and Murugan and Griffiths, all had a hand in intercepting it. Though you didn't know it, you were doing our firm – England itself, perhaps – a valuable service. It remains to bring the guilty person to justice.'

We were silent.

'Do we go to the police?' Harold asked.

'No use going to Sergeant Cogger at the local police station, I think,' said Mr Woods. 'Nobody's committed that sort of a crime. The fellow didn't even steal the firm's paper. He seems to have supplied his own.'

Mouse burst out, 'But, Dad, if it's sabotage – if he's mucking about with the instruments – he might kill you! It's murder!'

'Difficult to prove, William,' his father said thoughtfully. 'Faulty workmanship's not a crime, yet.'

'Don't we shoot spies, sir?' Griffiths demanded.

'We're not at war yet, either,' Parker said. 'And Shorts is not a secret military site.'

'It would be, in Hitler's Germany,' said Harold. 'That's why they go in for the cloak-and-dagger stuff over here.'

I said, 'The gentleman had an overcoat and a walking stick,' and they laughed again, except for Parker, who spoke seriously.

'If we could prove he was handing over information to a foreign power, that would be different. *Who* was supposed to collect the packet from the archway? Worth following that up, eh, Woods?'

Mr Woods nodded. 'We could make inquiries round the cathedral.'

'You said the Dean saw this man, Murugan.' Griffiths shot the words at me.

'Yes,' I answered.

'When was that?' Mr Woods demanded.

'That Sunday evening,' I told him.

Mr Woods moved purposefully towards the telephone again.

'Oh no, Daddy, not the *Dean*,' Barbara protested, but feebly. 'He – he may be saying his prayers.'

But Mr Woods soon got the call through, and immediately a powerful voice came back through the receiver, the voice that made the echoes of the cathedral ring.

'Dean here.'

'Shorts Brothers, Geoffrey Woods speaking,' Mr Woods boomed back. 'I trust I'm not interrupting matters of ecclesiastical importance –'

'Not at all! I was reading a thriller,' the voice returned.

'Well, then, perhaps you'd be interested in a minor mystery we're concerned about, Dr Wigmore. Do you understand what I mean by a *dead drop?*'

'Oh dear, not something that has happened to one of your aeroplanes, I hope.'

'No. Not yet, anyway – look, Dr Wigmore, I'd rather not say any more on the telephone. Do you think we could drop round?'

'By all means! Come and have a cup of tea. You will be most welcome. I must say that you have got me thoroughly intrigued.'

After some more polite remarks Mr Woods hung up and turned to us.

'Well, we've got the Dean intrigued. Who'd like to come with me? Tea at the Deanery.'

This time nobody wanted to go. Tea at the Deanery wasn't a treat. So when the big car came round with the chauffeur it drove Barbara and William home, then went on with Mr Woods and me to the Deanery. A parlour-maid opened the door and showed us into the drawing-room. A fire of logs, pictures of mountains and animals on the walls, a thick carpet. I could only think of the mud from Wouldham Marshes on my shoes.

The Very Reverend the Dean of Rochester was sitting in a comfortable chair covered with flowery stuff. He got to his feet and greeted us warmly. Mr Woods introduced me.

'Charming to meet one of our younger brethren, from India's coral strand. And how you must be missing your sunshine, eh? Here, sit by the fire on this stool. Now, Woods, I am all agog. So seldom that we churchmen can be of practical help to you men of affairs. What's all this about a – er, a *dead drop?*'

'If I've got it right, it's a term of international espionage, Dr Wigmore. An agent has secret information. He leaves it in a pre-arranged hiding place. A colleague comes and collects it later. That's a dead drop, and perhaps it's happening near the cathedral.'

'In *our precinct?* Dear me, I thought such things only took place between the covers of a thriller. Tell me more, my dear fellow! Tell me more!'

Mr Woods went quickly over the story of the *gentleman*, the packet, and the suspected fitter at the factory. I was glad I didn't have to tell it this time. In this very respectable drawing-room, I began to think it must be nonsense again.

'And Murugan here says you were the only other person to see the suspect that Sunday evening, Dr Wigmore,' Mr Woods finished. The Dean looked at me.

'Was I indeed? Can you tell me exactly which Sunday this was?'

I had to shake my head. One Sunday in Rochester is very much like another.

'You can't perhaps remember the collect for the day?'

What was he talking about now? *Collect* – it rhymed with *rollicked*. I used to think it had something to do with the bag that came round in church for our pennies. Actually it was a special prayer in the prayer-book. Why should I remember it, and how would it help if I did?

But suddenly I had a vision of Mouse kneeling giggling in the Lady Chapel, and I remembered.

'Stir up, O Lord, the plenteous fruit of thy people . . .' I said, and stuck.

The Dean gave a delighted laugh.

'Well done, young man! Not quite according to the Book of Common Prayer. But it was Stir-Up Sunday, was it? The day your mother mixes her Christmas pudding.' I must have looked blank, because he hastily went on. 'But perhaps not in India, eh?'

It was like the Headmaster talking about cakes and candles and birthdays – more of a mystery to me than this spy story.

'Would you mind pulling that bell in the corner?' was the next thing the Dean said to me. Not sure that I was doing the right thing, I pulled the silken tassel that hung from the ceiling, and half expected the cathedral steeple to break out into peals. After a while the parlour-maid came in.

'Serve tea, would you, please, Doris?' the Dean requested. 'And please bring me last year's engagement diary from my study.'

Tea soon came in on a big silver tray, and the maid fetched a leather-bound book. I got a slice of seedcake, which I didn't like. The Dean looked at his diary.

'Twenty-fifth Sunday after Trinity,' he murmured. 'Yes, indeed, I may well have been at my own front door at nightfall that evening. I don't seem to have been anywhere else.'

At last, no less a person than the Dean of Rochester was going to support my story!

'But I haven't the foggiest recollection of seeing anyone at all, I fear,' he added. The seedcake stuck in my throat. That was that.

Even Mr Woods looked a bit embarrassed, though he can't have felt as silly as I did. There might have been an awkward silence. But the Dean seemed to feel called upon to give us a little sermon.

'As a man of peace I confess I am reluctant to think of espionage in Rochester or of imminent war with Germany. I have German friends, and I find them charming and civilized people. Why, only last month I met an erudite Herr Doktor in the precinct. He was passionately interested in ecclesiastical architecture – strangely enough, he was taking measurements of that same archway you were talking about.'

Mr Woods, who had begun to fidget, now leaned forward in his chair.

'What was this German's job, do you know?'

'Job?' asked Dr Wigmore. 'Oh yes, somebody did tell me. A very respectable job in the German Embassy. A military attaché.'

'Good God!' exclaimed Mr Woods – and upset a teacup on to his lap.

I was very glad it wasn't me – such language and behaviour in the Dean's drawing-room! But Mr Woods seemed to have something else on his mind as he made his apologies and said his good-byes. He was silent in the back of the car, but I dared to ask him a question.

'What is *military attaché?*'

'A spy who's so important that we can't touch him. You're not to say a word to anybody!'

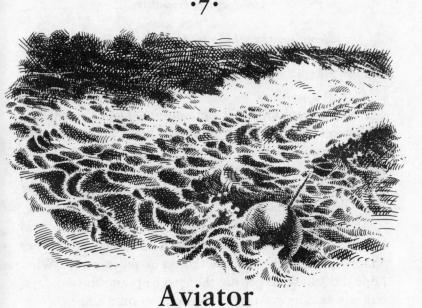

7

Aviator

I was in D.

D for Detention. It was a punishment for bad work or bad behaviour. Not lateness this time. I'd been moved up to a form that was doing chemistry. I'd gone into the chemmy lab for the first time, and there was this funny-shaped bottle in a glass cupboard. The bottle had a rubber tube coming from it with a clip on it. All I'd done was to fiddle with this clip and the most terrible smell had come out. *Pooh!* Now I knew why chemistry was called 'Stinks'. The master had thought I'd done it on purpose, so here I was, shut up for an extra hour this afternoon, with bored day-boys who wanted to go home. But it didn't make much difference to me.

I had been given Revision Exercises in *Godfrey and Price* to do. They were very dull and had taken no time at all, but I had to stay for the full hour. I looked through the book for something more interesting. After a lot of searching I did find one example about an aeroplane!

> *In attempting the 5 km speed record, an airman flew 5 km in 2 mins., 48 secs. Express this in miles per hour, given 1 km = 0.621 mile.*

I wasn't even sure what 'km' meant. Then I remembered kilometres – the French used them, didn't they? How fast did this record-breaker go? 107 kilometres an hour? But how fast was that? 66 miles an hour?

But at 66 miles an hour it would take – what? Half a week to fly to Madras.

Anyhow, what difference did it make to me? Here was I, shut up in a dusty classroom. There was my brother Shanmugam, in prison six thousand miles away. What hope did I have of getting there to help him in two days, half a week, or even in a month or so on a ship?

There was a knock on the door of the Detention Room. A boy came in and spoke to the master in charge. The master spoke to me.

'Murugan, you're to go to the Headmaster in his house.'

The other boys made round eyes and *ooo* mouths, as if they were horrified at the fate that awaited me. They made me feel it must be bad – to be summoned out of school hours to the Headmaster's house!

I had to go past the Deanery and through The Vines. All sorts of guilty thoughts went through my head on the way. It had all gone wrong, I was sure, and now I was in real trouble. That's what came of giving everything away to Mr Woods, and to the Dean – who obviously didn't believe a word of it.

There was a way through the boarding house to the place where the Headmaster lived, but it felt all wrong to be going through, alone. There were voices coming from the other side of a closed door. I thought it was the

Headmaster's drawing-room. Was I supposed to knock at it? I stood there, wretchedly.

A loud, confident male voice was speaking. I didn't think I'd heard it before.

'Let the lad choose. He might like a decent cricket bat, even a bicycle. We would have a little presentation ceremony and he'll have his picture in the papers.'

Who could they be talking about? I thought I'd better wait until they'd finished. Then I recognized the Old Man's voice.

'Oh dear, does there have to be publicity?'

'My dear Headmaster,' the other voice boomed. 'This sort of thing keeps the Idea of Empire in the minds of our young people. There can surely be no harm in that.'

'They're taking a long time finding him,' came another voice. It was Mr Woods. I felt a little better. I liked Mouse's father.

The Headmaster's voice said, 'I'm afraid he has the reputation for being late.'

Ooops – it was me they were talking about! And I was keeping them waiting! I knocked on the door, was told to come in, and crept through the doorway.

A large gentleman in an expensive dark suit seemed to be occupying most of the carpet. Mr Woods and the Head were the only other ones.

'This is Murugan,' said the Old Man, and a very large soft hand shook mine. Then the other two looked at the Old Man, and the Old Man silently picked up a newspaper from a writing-table. It was a very dull-looking paper with no pictures on the front, but he opened it and showed me a headline.

MILITARY ATTACHÉ
PERSONA NON GRATA

'I don't suppose you have seen *The Times*, Murugan,' the Old Man said with a smile that I didn't understand. 'Do you understand what it says there?'

A language test was the last thing I'd expected. I mean, I only knew Tamil and something of one or two other Indian languages. This looked like French and Latin. I guessed wildly.

'The attached soldier is not a nice person.'

They laughed. But people are always laughing at me. The large man spoke.

'Don't you know you've caused a high-ranking foreigner to be expelled from the country?'

Expelled? That was a terrible word. *Outer darkness – gnashing of teeth.*

'I didn't mean to, sir,' was all that I could say. What had I done? But they laughed again.

The large man boomed on, but I only slowly began to understand what he was saying.

'Young fellow, by your keen observation and initiative you have helped to unmask a plot that might have done incalculable damage to our company, the kingdom, and the Empire itself. I'm here on behalf of Short Brothers to express our appreciation.'

It sounded like a public speech. Was he talking to me? I didn't know what to say. I was glad when Mr Woods did some explaining.

'You see, Murugan, your mysterious gentleman in The Vines did turn out to be our fitter Webber – or rather a German spy called Weber. And he'd been giving information to the German Embassy about Chatham Dockyard, too. I'm afraid Webber's given us the slip, but at least we've got rid of the military attaché. Mr Short would like you to choose something as a reward for your help, to show how grateful we are.'

So I'd been right all the time. And I could choose a reward!

I couldn't think, but I said what was in my mind – what had been in my mind for weeks, months.

'Thank you, sir. I would like to fly to India.'

There was a bit of a silence. Had I asked too much – a hundred-pound trip? Weren't they as grateful as all that?

It was the Headmaster who spoke first.

'Your guardian would scarcely wish you to be absent in term-time, Murugan. And – have you anyone to go to in India?'

Yes, sir, my wicked anti-British brother. But of course I didn't say that.

Mr Short turned to Mr Woods.

'Woods, is there any reason why the boy shouldn't go up locally on one of our trial flights? It would show the public how safe our machines are.'

'Are you so sure there *is* no danger?' the Headmaster asked, doubtfully.

'None at all, on one of our routine test flights, Head-master,' Mr Woods said. 'Why not, eh, Murugan?'

And – well, that was how it came to be arranged. It wasn't what I wanted at all. I wanted a quick trip to India, yes, but I didn't want to fly for the sake of flying. I didn't want to fly at all if I could help it. It was just something else to worry about.

But there I was, about a week later, shivering on the windy slipway of the Shorts factory. And it wasn't only the icy wind off the Medway that made me shiver. I had agreed to go up into the sky in that crazy contraption moored in the river. If I had to fly, why couldn't I go up in something safe – like a balloon?

Harold, the younger pilot, was standing near me.

'Have you been up before?' he asked me cheerfully.

I shook my head.

'It'll be a thrill for you, then. Parker says it's okay if you sit up in Mercury with me. I shan't have a lot to do, just watch things. We shan't be separating from Maia, and he'll be doing all the flying.'

A man with a camera came along the jetty.

'Can we have a few pictures while you're all in one piece?' *Click, click.* 'There'll be one of our reporters along afterwards, if you come back safe.' *Click, click.* 'Where's the best place to catch you coming to bits in the air? Look 'appy!' *Click, click.*

I wished he wouldn't talk like that.

'We are *not* attempting separation today.' The senior pilot, Parker, was trying to keep his temper. 'It's all been explained to your news editor. This is just a routine test flight.'

'I've never snapped a plane crash yet,' the photographer grinned. 'But you never know your luck.'

He took some more pictures of us getting into the boat and going out to Mercury-Maia. Then I saw I had to clamber up the side of the flying-boat, up the Meccano that held the two planes together, and up into the seaplane above. There were footholds and handholds, but the whole thing was rocking gently on the water. It was nearly too much for me – but what would it be like up in the sky?

We squeezed into the cramped cabin, and Harold strapped me into a seat. I could see dozens of little dials and switches.

'That's for the co-pilot,' he said. 'But we're only going to the mouth of the Thames and back, so you won't need to do much navigating!'

I was already gripping the sides of my seat, and he grinned.

'You don't have to hang on yet. It'll take hours to check the instruments. I'll show you the trickiest one first – whatever you do, don't touch it! Look down there.'

On the floor between his seat and mine was a lever with a red knob on it. It was at one end of a slot, marked SECURE. The other end of the slot was marked DIS-ENGAGE.

'There's only one mechanism in the world like that. We're still not sure it will work. We know Maia can fly alone, we know Mercury can fly alone, we know they can fly together. We *don't* know what will happen when we release that lever. As it is now, it's holding the two aircraft together. Take that pin out and pull it back to *disengage* – and what have you got?'

I looked at him round-eyed.

'Nobody knows exactly, though we've done tests on models. You've got two large aircraft flying a few inches apart at a hundred miles an hour. Do you know what I mean by turbulence?'

I shook my head.

'Look at the tide flowing past that mooring buoy out there. See how the water swirls round behind it? The air does the same sort of thing round an aircraft, though you can't see it. But just what will it do between the two aircraft, so close together?'

He held one spread hand over the other, shaking them up and down expressively. I could see what he meant. I shut my eyes.

'But that's not your worry, nor ours, today. We'll just go for a quick flip and back again, all in one piece.'

A quick flip. That was all right. It couldn't be too quick for me. Let's get it over with.

But it was hours before anything happened. Harold fixed us both up with headphones and microphones, and we could hear Parker speaking from Maia down below. Then they went on and on, the two of them, pressing little switches and saying whether little coloured lights came on. Harold was too busy to explain what they all meant, though he did break off to speak to me once.

'It's not all go, being a test pilot. Mostly wait and see!'

I sat there, wishing that I had chosen a cricket bat. Or a bicycle. How long would it take to get to India on a bicycle? At ten miles an hour? Twenty-five days? But that would mean never stopping to eat or sleep, or mend a puncture . . .

An almighty roar that nearly shook me out of my seat! My heart almost stopped beating. I looked wildly round and out through the window.

One of Maia's engines had started up. Only one. Seven more to come. What would it be like when all eight were going?

Stupefying! I stopped thinking and I stopped feeling. I wasn't even afraid any longer. I watched the grey little houses of Strood begin to wheel past as we turned up-river, then the wintry woods of Cobham. And over the other side of the water that must be Borstal where the bad lads were sent, and The Alps. At least this was better than freezing on the football pitch. But of course we weren't flying yet. We were just a crazy craft taxiing up the river.

Opposite Cuxton the landscape began to spin again. We were turning round for the take-off. I gripped the sides of my seat again – as if that would make any difference to what might happen to me! But the roar of the eight engines died down to a growl, and there was a lot more talk, quiet but tense, between the two pilots.

I did understand one thing that Harold said.

'Are you sure we haven't got Geoff Woods hanging on to my floats this time?'

I was glad they could make a bit of a joke.

Harold moved levers, and all eight engines grew to a deafening din, louder than ever. He found time to turn to me with a grin and a nod. This must be it. For the first time I was going to leave this friendly earth, on which I'd lived for – for however long it was – and I was going to take to the skies.

I gripped my seat and shut my eyes. Then I did a heroic thing. I opened them again. Whatever was going to happen to me, I might as well watch and make the best of it.

We were racing along past the mud of Wouldham Marshes. There ahead on the right was the castle, towering over the river bank. The cathedral ought to be hidden behind it – but I was seeing the cathedral over the castle. How could I be?

We had left the water and I hadn't even noticed! The castle keep and the cathedral spire were below us. The cement works of Frindsbury and Upnor rushed to meet us. But now we were well up, over the chalk quarries and the hills beyond.

Words came from Parker, and Harold eased back his throttle levers. The roar of the engines quietened down a little. The misty horizon tilted gently – and ahead, suddenly, it seemed there was no land beneath us. Only rippling water, mudbanks, and a great empty space where the grey misty sky met a grey misty sea.

So this was flying! When Harold turned to give me another grin I was even able to smile back.

Parker's voice came over the headphones of the intercom.

'Stand by for pre-separation trial. Okay, Harold? We'll settle her steady on separation course and speed, controls at the agreed state. Fly like that for thirty seconds only.

We will not – repeat *not* – separate. Then revert to present state. Understood?'

'Understood,' replied Harold.

He made some careful adjustments to the controls and he watched the dials with intense concentration. We flew along quietly and steadily. Nothing much seemed to be happening. Parker's voice came over again.

'How's it going, Harold? Any stress up there?'

'Going like a dream, old boy.' He read some figures off the dials.

'Fine!' came Parker's voice. 'I think we can report the trial successfu –'

His voice broke off in mid-word. Something had made me look at the floor. I was watching that red knob smoothly sliding from one end of its slot to the other, as if a ghostly hand was working it. It stopped at DIS-ENGAGE.

'Hello, Parker?' Harold was saying, with only a little bit of anxiety in his voice. 'Hello, can you hear me? The intercom seems to have failed. Hello, hello, are you there?' His eyes were on the instrument panel.

I looked out through the perspex, down to where the broad wings of Maia ought to be.

They weren't there.

'He's gone!' I shouted into my microphone. I must have deafened Harold. He looked out through the perspex, looked down at the release switch, glared at me in fury.

'What did you *do*?'

'I didn't do anything!' Luckily he believed me.

He turned his attention to the flight controls – and then he burst out laughing.

'We've done it, youngster! We've done it! We didn't mean to, but we did it! And we didn't even notice we'd done it!'

He banked the aircraft round, and there, well below us, was Maia plodding ahead on an even keel.

'Do you think *he's* noticed?' Harold crowed. 'We haven't even got the radio going – didn't think we'd need it. We'll have to show ourselves.'

The horizon tipped upwards and I got the feeling of going down a slide, leaving my tummy behind. We were diving down ahead of Maia. The horizon levelled off, but then it tipped quickly sideways and seesawed back again. What was happening? I looked anxiously at Harold.

'It's okay,' he said. 'Just waggling our wings at old Parky. Better not risk a victory roll, I suppose. We'll go home now.'

He banked steeply round, and there below us were the smoky Medway Towns: Rochester, Chatham and Gillingham. There was the cathedral and the castle, and the thin silvery strip of the river. Over the factory chimneys of Snodland we banked round again, and now the narrow river was coming up to meet us. I was gripping my seat again. What I feared now was drowning. What was to stop us plunging straight through the surface of the water?

The slopes of the valley were whizzing past. A beautiful spray of water sprang up from our floats on either side. We slowed, settled on the water, and taxied gently towards Shorts' slipways.

I'd been up, I'd come down, and I was still alive. I was an aviator!

There was a motorboat coming out to meet us, with Mr Woods, the photographer and a man with a notebook. Mr Woods looked anxious and angry. As soon as the cabin hatch was opened he shouted up to us.

'What the hell happened?'

Harold poked his head out and grinned happily.

'Gremlins!' he said.

Well, that's how I got into the papers. Of course they got my name wrong; they always do. This was how they put it into the *Kent Messenger*.

FLYING MASCOT
MAKES MERCURY RISE

Master J. Gremlin, of Murugan, India, had the flight of his life in Shorts' controversial composite aircraft – which came unstuck in mid-air. 'He was our lucky mascot,' said test pilot Harold Singer. 'I wish we'd flown all the way to India,' was plucky Gremlin's comment.

But I don't think it was gremlins who tampered with that release catch. I think the *gentleman* was still around.

8

Stowaway

Red sails in the sunset,
Far over the sea,
Oh, carry my loved one
Home safely to me!

The music tailed off in a mournful moan.

Barbara said, 'For goodness' sake wind it up, Mouse!'

William furiously wound the handle of the little square clockwork gramophone. The singer perked up, but sounded a bit husky.

'It needs a new gramophone needle,' said Barbara.

'You need a new record,' William said.

'I like that record,' Barbara said. So did I. I liked sitting in the cosy room in the Woods' house, which they still called *the nursery*. I liked being asked home by the Woods family. I liked William. I liked Barbara, especially.

She was looking at that newspaper.

'Do you really want to fly to India?' she asked me.

'Yes,' I said. 'They asked me what I wanted as a reward and I said I wanted to fly to India. I – I want to see my family. But it was very kind of them to let me have that short trip.'

'They asked you what you wanted and then they didn't give it to you?' she demanded.

'Yes, I asked too much.'

Barbara threw down the paper angrily.

'I think it's a *swizz!* I think they're being *mean!*'

'Perhaps it is not possible, what I asked.'

'But Mercury is going to fly to India,' she said.

William asked her scornfully, 'Who told you that one, Bats?'

'Oh, I get to hear things, at home,' she tossed her head. 'I'm pretty sure of this one.'

We sat and listened to that record again from the beginning. Or, rather, I didn't listen. My mind was churning. Mercury was flying all the way to India. Madras in a couple of days, Mr Woods had said. So did all my calculations – but no, it was no use my thinking about it. I'd had my reward.

Barbara lifted the arm off the gramophone.

'You'll have to be a stowaway,' she said.

'What is stow-a-way?' I could hardly even say the word. I was still having trouble with my English W's, and this word had two in it.

'Oh, he doesn't even know the *word!* Sometimes I think you're useless, Mugwumps!'

I turned away from her, pretending to feel very hurt. But I wasn't. She was talking to me as she talked to her own brother. That made us equals.

'Sorry!' she said, and she gave my knee a quick pat. 'Look. There's Mercury down on the river. It'll fly to India *tomorrow!* All you've got to do is get on board and stay there. I bet *I* could!'

It seemed simple. Too simple?

'What do you think, Mouse?' she turned to her brother.

'I suppose he could. But it's term-time.'

'Oh, *bloody term-time!*' she swore. I didn't like her using such words.

'It's running away from school,' said Mouse. 'They can expel you for that.'

'People who run away don't want to stay, do they? All we've got to do is get up early. We can pack you some pie or something from the larder. You won't need a lot of food for less than two days. Then we can take the dinghy out and pretend we're going for an early morning row. We'll get you on board somehow.' She was speaking quietly now, hatching her plot.

'Suppose it doesn't work?' Mouse said.

'If it doesn't work, it doesn't work. But it'll work if we don't funk it.'

I had the feeling that things were out of my hands, with this forceful girl in charge. I couldn't believe it would happen, even though I wanted it to. I just went along with Barbara's detailed plans. She would borrow Cook's alarm clock while she wasn't looking – though I was sure I wouldn't be able to sleep a wink myself. I would have to put on all the warm clothes I'd got, because they thought the baggage-hold would get very cold. The family had a little boat down by the river, and they would row me out to Mercury-Maia, moored in the stream. And that was it.

I felt I ought to go round saying good-bye to everybody, as I'd done when I left India, but of course I couldn't. We had to pretend to Mr and Mrs Woods that nothing was happening. It was difficult to keep talking about other things. When Barbara and William asked to go to bed early, Mrs Woods looked quite worried.

'You're not sickening for something, are you?' she demanded.

Mouse and I were to sleep in the same bedroom. Or, rather, we agreed we would rest in our beds and keep awake until it was time to go. I looked in my little suitcase to see what warm clothes I'd brought. If I'd known I was packing for such an adventure I could have brought sports sweaters and things. But I'd have to make do with a spare woolly vest and two pairs of socks.

'You could wear your pajama underneath your suit,' Mouse suggested.

'My pyjamas,' I corrected him. We both giggled, remembering my first night at school. We got into our beds and Mouse turned off the light.

'We can't leave the light on all night,' he said. 'Mum and Dad might suspect something.'

We settled down in the dark to our murmured conversation.

'Even if it does work, won't you get into trouble, you and Barbara?' I asked.

'I dare say. But they can't eat us.'

'Won't they search for me, as soon as they notice I'm missing?'

'Mmm. We'll think of some story. I'll say you went back to school for something – for your cough medicine.'

'Say good-bye to Stodge for me, when I'm gone,' I asked him. 'Tell him I'll bring him back some burphy.'

'What's burpy?' I heard him giggle in the dark.

'A kind of sweet. It will make him even fatter.'

'So you *are* coming back, then?'

'How can I tell? I may not get another free trip.'

'I suppose you may not want to, once you're in India. Do you have to go to school there?'

'You are lucky if your parents can send you to school.'

'I don't think it's lucky. Anyway, hasn't your father got enough money?'

It was strange – we knew each other quite well now, but we hardly ever talked about these things.

'My father is dead,' I told him. He was silent for a bit.

'Sorry. Was he a rich man?'

'He had a catamaran.'

'What's that?'

'A kind of boat.'

'So he was a shipowner?'

'Not exactly. A catamaran is five logs tied together, and a sail. My father went fishing in the monsoon, and never came back. That's why my mother became a Christian.'

'Sorry – I don't understand.'

'My father believed in the Indian gods – Vishnu, and Krishna, and Ganesha the elephant god, and Murugan after whom I am named. But they did not look after him well, did they? Someone told my mother that Jesus would look after her and her sons better. And it is true, isn't it? Look, I am having this excellent education in Rochester! But my brother needs my help and I must go to him.'

How much should I tell him about my brother? Would he understand? But something about William's steady breathing told me that he was already asleep. And with nobody to keep me awake, I went off to sleep myself.

Deep, deep sleep. Some confused dreams, about a flying-boat made of logs tied together with rope. A man like a black bat in a wading-suit was untying the ropes . . .

Someone was shaking my arm as I tried to snuggle down into my supersoft warm bed. Was I late for school breakfast, for shoe-polishing, for a day of lessons? I opened my eyes to darkness, except for the wavering beam of a little electric torch. A figure was bending over me, and the light fell on a pair of riding jodhpurs and thick socks.

'Wake up! Wake *up!*' came Barbara's sharp whisper. 'It's twenty to five.'

The air in the bedroom was cold. Oh, no! It all came back to me, yesterday's silly plot about flying to India. But it was one thing to hatch a plot in a cosy nursery. Did they really think I was going to get up in the freezing dark and *do* it? That was something quite different. I groaned and wriggled back under the blankets.

But Barbara was over by William's bed now, giving him a shake.

'Come *on*, William! Get yourself dressed and see that Murugan does too. I'll be down in the kitchen.'

At school William was always one of the slowest in the morning. But at his sister's bidding he had switched on his torch and rolled out of bed. Now he was over by mine, pulling all the bedclothes off.

'But I'm not going!' I protested.

'Rot!' he said. 'Get dressed!'

It was no use arguing with these two. They were determined to start their adventure, whatever I felt about it. I got up and put on as many clothes as I could find.

By the light of his torch William and I crept very quietly downstairs past his parents' bedroom, and down to the kitchen. There was a smell of cold grease, and Barbara's torchlight flickering about as she put things into a brown paper bag on the scrubbed kitchen table. William's torch shone on the dog, looking up and wagging his tail hopefully.

'Cold cooked sausages, chocolate biscuits, and an orange,' Barbara whispered. 'I'm afraid it's all I can find. Hadn't you better have something to eat before you go?'

Impossible! My mouth was as dry as if I was dying of thirst, and my stomach was churning. I drank two glasses of water at the kitchen tap, and stuffed the paper bag into my overcoat pocket. William handed me another little bag.

'What's that?' Barbara asked.

'Survival kit,' William whispered. 'Pencil and paper, a pen knife, a torch, a piece of string and some money. It's a lucky rupee Dad gave me – that's Indian, isn't it?'

I thanked him and put the bag into my other pocket. My baggage for a six-thousand-mile journey! I still couldn't believe it was happening.

Barbara had an iron key in her hand. She moved towards the back door. 'Let's go, then,' she said quietly. 'Come on, Wat, boy!'

'He's not taking the dog to India!' William protested.

'Idiot!' Barbara hissed. 'If we leave Wat behind he'll bark to come with us and wake up the whole house. We've got to take him.'

She unlocked and opened the back door, and the east wind hit us. I wrapped my school scarf round my head and face. As we stole across the back lawn the stars were twinkling overhead. There was a glare in the city sky from the all-night street-lighting, but no sign of dawn. My heart began to pump with excitement. After all, this *was* an adventure.

'Oars!' William suddenly hissed in the silence.

'Eh?' Barbara queried.

'In the summer house,' William whispered. 'We'll need oars, for the dinghy.' He went off to the other side of the lawn and came back after a time with a bundle of long things in his arms. He gave me two oars to carry. Barbara shone a light on the other things.

'We don't need *fishing rods*, stupid!' she hissed.

'I thought we'd better take them.'

'Oh, all *right*, then, take them.'

From the way they were snapping at each other I could see they were as nervous as I was.

We went out through the garden gate and took the footpath down to the river. There were street-lights near the factory, and beyond them the river was vast and dark.

'There she is,' William hissed, pointing with his fishing rods towards the water. We stopped on the slope. I could just make out the crazy Meccano structure of Mercury-Maia, moored in the stream. How could that thing fly me to India? I must be dreaming, and I would soon wake up.

On the riverside road to the factory our footsteps echoed back to us from brick walls. William flapped his hand to us, signalling us to stop. We halted and listened. Footsteps, heavy and slow, continued to sound. They weren't ours. Round a corner came a tall dark figure in a cape. A policeman.

Oh, well, that was that. What were you supposed to say? *It's a fair cop?* We'd all get sent straight to Borstal – though perhaps not Barbara.

The policeman paced steadily towards us and shone an electric lantern on our faces. Barbara's bright voice rang out.

'Hello, it's Constable Heaver! Keeping a good watch on the factory, Constable Heaver?'

'Well I never! It's Miss Woods, isn't it?' said the policeman. 'And young master William.' He stared suspiciously at my face, all wrapped up, but I decided not to unwrap it. 'What may you be doing, out so early?'

'Daddy always likes an early start for a fishing trip,' Barbara chirped. 'If you see him with a bucket of maggots, tell him we've gone on to the boat, will you, please?'

The constable looked at William. 'Got the rest of your gear, I see. All right, Miss Barbara, I'll keep a look out for your Dad.' He stooped stiffly to pat the dog. 'Don't get up to mischief before he comes, will you?' And with a last suspicious glance at me he went on his way.

When we'd got far enough in the other direction Bats and Mouse exploded into relieved giggles.

'Bucket of maggots!' William spluttered. 'The lies you tell, Bats!'

'I didn't tell any lies,' Barbara insisted. 'I said *if* he met Daddy with a bucket of maggots – well, he'd know what to say.'

What a family! They had no respect for anybody, not even policemen.

'It was my fishing rods that made him believe you, though,' William said.

'I suppose it *was* a good idea to bring them,' his sister gave way.

Away from the factory there was a little jetty where shadowy dinghies were tied up. In midstream the dancing water reflected starlight and the street-lamps of Strood. But at this end of the jetty – the two torches shone down on boats stuck in black mud.

'Oh, *no*!' The laughter died out of Barbara's voice. 'You didn't think of the tide, did you, William?'

'Nor did you!' William snapped back. 'It's right out. What do we do now? Wait for it to come in?'

I looked down at the slimy, smelly mud, sorry for my friends and their plans that had gone wrong. Perhaps *I* should have thought of the tide. It's easy enough to calculate high water if you know when the moon rises . . . But perhaps we could go back to bed now.

William had wandered on to the end of the jetty. Now he was calling back to us.

'Come on! There's water at this end. And someone's boat.'

Barbara and the dog ran to the end of the jetty. I followed. They were shining their torches down on to a heavy, clumsy-looking dinghy tied up to the bottom of an iron ladder. It was floating in a little muddy channel.

'Are you going to steal a boat?' I protested.

'People do borrow boats,' Mouse said. 'We'll get it back, I suppose.'

'It'll do,' Barbara said, and began to climb down the ladder. She pulled the boat towards her by the rope, and got in.

'Pass down the oars and things,' she ordered. We did that easily enough.

'What about the dog?' William asked from the jetty.

'Oh, why did we have to bring him?' Barbara groaned.

'It wasn't my idea,' her brother snapped.

'Get half-way down the ladder, Mouse,' Barbara ordered. 'Murugan can pass him down to you and you can pass him to me.'

That was easier said than done. I don't think that dog liked the idea of water at all. He wriggled and whined and I didn't know what to hold on by. William nearly dropped him, and he yelped as Barbara dumped him in the boat.

'*Shut up, Wat!*' said Barbara between clenched teeth. 'Next time we'll leave you *behind!*'

Next time? I wondered how often they thought they'd do this sort of thing.

It was my turn to go down that ladder. As I got to the bottom Barbara called out another order.

'Let go the painter!'

'I beg your pardon?' I had to say.

I was hanging on to the slimy iron ladder, and it was freezing my fingers.

'The *rope*, Mugwumps,' William said. 'Undo it!'

My fingers struggled with the soggy rope in the cold iron ring. At last it came undone and flopped into the water. William hung on to the ladder as I got into the boat. My foot went into an inch or two of icy water sloshing around in the bottom.

'Can you row, Murugan?' Barbara asked me.

Well, yes, I wasn't a fisherman's son for nothing. I had helped to man the big rowing-sweeps on the river boats at home. You stood up facing forwards and pushed on the handle of the long oar. So I took an oar and, standing in the dinghy, looked for somewhere to lodge it. The little boat rocked.

'For goodness' sake sit *down!*' Barbara hissed. 'If you don't know anything about rowing, say so!'

I wasn't even sure I liked this girl any more.

She snatched the oar from me and sat down facing the back of the boat. William took the other oar and did the same on the other side. It seemed a funny way to move a boat – they couldn't even see where they were going. Did *they* know what they were doing?

But it seemed to work. There was just enough water in that narrow channel to float the boat out towards the main stream. Then we were out on the choppy water, and brother and sister had to work hard together to keep the boat moving against wind and tide. All I could do was keep my eyes on the shadowy outline of Mercury-Maia, and tell them 'This way a bit!' or 'That way a bit!' to keep them on course.

'Are you sure you can see it?' Barbara panted, between strokes.

'Yes, it's got a light on,' I told her. 'Do you think that means there's someone there?'

'Don't think so,' she puffed. 'They've got to have a light – to stop boats bumping into it.'

But after a while the light went out. Somebody must have switched it off. So there must be somebody there. I told Barbara.

'What do we do if there *is* someone there?' I asked Barbara.

'Carry on fishing,' she said, saving her breath.

We were getting nearer. The black shape of Mercury-Maia merged with the mass of Rochester Bridge behind it. I couldn't be sure which I was looking at. Was that a dark figure walking along Maia's wing? Or was it somebody on the bridge?

The darkness and the reflections of the lamps on the bridge kept playing tricks with my eyes. Wasn't that a small black shape moving away from Maia's hull, about the size of the boat we were in?

'Can you stop rowing for a bit?' I asked.

Barbara stopped and William copied her.

'Not for long,' she panted. 'We'll get blown backwards. What's the matter?'

'Listen!' I said. 'Can't you hear oars?'

We listened.

'It's the water lapping against the flying-boat,' William said. But the dog, in the front of the boat with his nose lifted, gave a single, muffled 'Woof!'

'*Shut up*, Wat!' Barbara hissed. 'Come on, Mouse, we're nearly there.'

A few minutes' more hard work by Barbara and William, and we were in the gloom under the giant wing of the flying-boat. William pulled in his oar and grabbed the strut of a float.

'Done it!' William said. But his sister hushed him to silence.

We listened again. The choppy waves flapped against the metal hull. The wind sighed between the struts and the criss-cross rigging. The whole top-heavy shape rocked gently on the water, and the float we were hanging on to plunged up and down. There was no sign of life.

Barbara broke silence.

'Well, Murugan –' she started, but her voice went all hoarse and she had to start again.

'Well, Murugan, we've done our bit. It's up to you now. Lucky you know your way up!'

I didn't want to be separated from her, or from my friend Mouse. Even the dog and the leaky boat seemed more friendly than this machine towering above us.

'Come up with me,' I said.

'All right, then,' she replied.

'Can I come too?' William asked.

'Somebody's got to stay with the dog and the boat,' she said firmly.

We pushed the boat across from the float to the side of the hull, and I tried to remember where the handholds were.

'Good-bye, Mugwumps,' said Mouse. 'Good luck!'

Oh, I wished they could all come with me, all the way.

'Good-bye, Mouse. Thank you for –' I couldn't finish. I had one foot on a step and the other in the boat. I swung over on to the hull.

Barbara was below me, shining her torch. But it had been bad enough climbing up the side of the plane in broad daylight with Harold to help me. Now it felt like climbing a tottering cathedral in the dark. Assisting Barbara made me forget my own fears, a little. Our cold hands clasped as I helped her up on to the wing.

All the time I had kept to myself one fear – or was it a hope? Surely they wouldn't leave two valuable aircraft alone like this, unlocked? It would be silly if we had gone to all this trouble and found ourselves locked out! On the other hand – we could go back to bed then.

But there was an odd knocking sound every time the planes rocked on the water. Barbara shone her torch along the side of Mercury where the sound seemed to come from.

The loading-door of Mercury's hold wasn't even *closed*. It lay a little bit open, bumping against the lock with every roll, just as if – *as if someone had left it like that in a hurry*.

'There!' Barbara breathed. 'I told you we could do it! They've even left the door open for us!'

I pulled the door wide open, got up over the sill, and pulled Barbara up after me. Then I knew there was no turning back.

Our feet made clanging echoes in Mercury's hold. We were out of that chill wind, but the metal walls were icy to touch. Barbara flashed the torch around – and gave a start, grabbing my arm. Dark forms, crouching at the far end of the hold! She kept the beam of light on them steadily.

'Sacks,' I whispered.

We went up to them. They were big sacks, some of them quite full, some nearly empty. Each one had a label and a string tied round its throat, and something stencilled on its side: GVIR. I knew what that stood for: King George the Sixth.

'Mail-bags,' said Barbara.

I looked at some of the labels: BOMBAY, NEW DELHI, CALCUTTA, MADRAS ... And for the first time I really believed in this journey I was to make. Those names were suddenly more real to me than anything else. They spelt *India*. If those bags were going there, I could too.

'Where's that penknife Mouse gave you?' Barbara asked. I felt in my pocket for the paper bag and the penknife, and handed it to Barbara. What was she going to do with it? I took out the torch too, which I'd forgotten about, and pushed forward the switch. A feeble red glow lit up the bulb, and faded out.

'Here, hold mine,' Barbara said. The thick strings were sealed with lead seals, and Barbara was cutting the string! The bag was not very full, and the label said MADRAS. She held open the top.

'Get in,' she said.

'What do you mean?'

'Get in the bag. Hide there and keep warm. The Royal Mail always gets through.'

I couldn't argue with that. I stepped into the bag, trying not to trample too much on the envelopes at the bottom. I gave the torch back to Barbara; she would need it to get down again. She gave me back the penknife. I stood there, holding the mail-bag with my left hand, like a pair of trousers half on and half off.

'Well, good-bye, Mugwumps,' she said. I saw her outstretched hand in the torchlight. I took hold of it and held it for longer than I had ever held it before.

'You will be all right, won't you?' she asked. There was a catch in her voice as if she was trying not to cry. A fine time for *her* to go all soft!

'Come with me,' I said. 'All the way!'

She hesitated for the briefest of moments.

'I wish I could. But I can't leave Mouse and Wat in the boat.'

'I shall be all right,' I said. 'Thank you for being so kind to me.'

'Oh, rot!' she exclaimed, just like her brother. English people don't like good-byes. She dropped my hand and said, 'Get right down into that bag. I'll just loop the string round the top. You'll be able to get it open.'

I got down into the dusty darkness of the mail-bag, on a cushion of envelopes. Barbara's knee poked into my back as she fastened the string outside – not too tight, I hoped. Then she seemed to be shifting the other sacks around.

'Just piling some more bags round you,' I heard her say. Then, 'Good-bye, Murugan! Good luck!'

I couldn't reply. I was already a speechless parcel, in the care of His Majesty's Royal Mail. I heard her feet cross the floor, and the door clang shut. She was gone.

And then I could only imagine things in the dark. Was that the sound of a motorboat coming through the water? Did I hear men's voices, and the voices of Barbara and William in reply? Had our plot been discovered, and would they come searching for me? Was I being a coward, lying there snugly while my friends were in trouble? Or would it make it worse for them if I showed myself?

I stayed where I was. No searchers came to look for me. The sounds seemed to fade away. I went back to the sleep I'd been missing since twenty to five that morning. What else was there for me to do?

9

Nonstop

I was having a nightmare. King George the Sixth, wearing his crown and a flying-suit, had tied me up in a parcel and dumped me in a sack, saying, 'The Royal Mail will get through.' But a monstrous figure in a dripping black rubber wading-suit and a gentleman's felt hat had stolen the sack and was burying me in the grave near the cathedral, cackling, 'Oh, no, it won't!' A heavy tombstone was coming down over my head . . .

I woke up and it was true! I struggled to pull bedclothes off my face and I couldn't do it! It was pitch dark, deathly cold, and I could hardly breathe, let alone move. I *was* buried in a sack!

Two voices argued inside my head, one panic-stricken, the other calmer.

Help! Help! Let me out! Get me out of this!
Lie still, relax, everything's going to plan.
I can't breathe!

There's enough air if you don't panic.
I'll freeze to death!
You're warmer in that bag than out of it.
I'll starve!
You've got food in your pocket.
It's so quiet! Nothing's happening!
'It's mostly wait and see' – remember?
They've forgotten all about the flight!
Barbara said they'll fly today. She knows.

Barbara! If anyone else had got me in this fix I'd be cursing that person. But Barbara was different. She was something nice to think about. My thoughts of Barbara didn't have any future – what could I ever mean to her? They didn't have much past either; I'd only known her for a few days. But what did time matter? My mind grew calmer and I went off into a doze again.

An almighty roar! I jerked into wakefulness again, and my two voices started up.

Whatever's that?
You remember. The first of Maia's engines starting up. Seven more to come.
Two ... three ... four ... five ... six ... seven ... eight! I shall never stand the noise!
You're lucky to be muffled in mail-bags.
If only I knew what was happening!
Try and remember. Taxiing down to the take-off. Strood and Cobham woods one side, Wouldham Marsh and Borstal –
I don't want to think about Borstal! What's happened to the engines?
Power on one side to turn us round. Ready for the take-off.

I don't like taking off! That's when accidents happen! If we crash they won't even look for me!

Take it easy. Full power on all engines.

I haven't got a seat belt! I haven't got a seat to hang on to! (I think I rolled up into a ball and clung on to my legs, like you're supposed to be before you're born) *Ooh – I'm leaving my tummy behind!*

That means we've taken off. And – see – nothing's gone wrong. We're airborne.

They haven't done the difficult bit yet, separating Mercury from Maia. Anything can happen! Harold said so.

They did it all right last time you flew.

I wasn't expecting it that time. What was that, right under my head? A loud clunk!

Must be the lock coming undone.

We're sort of juddering and swaying! What's going to happen?

Nothing. Listen – Maia's engines fading away. Just Mercury's engines now. Four Napier Rapiers, 340 horsepower each, taking us all the way to India.

They're only gadgets, those engines. The men who put them together, they ride to work on rusty bicycles. You think they'll keep us in the sky till next Wednesday?

Even if they can't, we've got floats. Anywhere there's a bit of water, we can come down.

What happens if we're over a mountain or a desert?

They must have thought of that. Do stop worrying.

I can't help worrying. I feel all empty inside.

You're just hungry. Have something to eat.

Both sides of my head thought this was a good idea. As soon as there was something to *do* I became one person again. I decided there was no reason to stay in that bag. I must get out.

Light, I must have light. I felt in my pocket for that torch, pulled it out, and pushed the switch. A feeble red glow lit up the bulb again, and faded out. I shook the torch, thumped it, even managed to take the end off in the dark and tightened the bulb. No use! It had been a kind thought of Mouse's to give me a torch – but a pity it had a dud battery!

It was difficult moving in that sack. I pushed my hand up to the top of it, as far as the string outside would let me. Panic again! It was too tight. I'd never fight my way out! No, my hand went through, and my other hand joined it and opened the bag above my head. I could feel another mail-bag on top of me. That was my nightmare! They had dumped more bags on top of me as I slept. Was I completely buried? Was there no space at the top of the hold?

I shoved madly at the bag above me, and it slid sideways, and there was air and empty darkness. I crawled up out of the pile and sat on top. It was very cold, and much noisier.

I explored the pile of mail-bags on hands and knees – and now I was sliding down the side of the heap on to the floor. I could stand up and stretch my legs – what a relief! The aircraft wobbled a little in the air and I fell sideways. My hand touched the side of the hold. I felt along the wall until I came to some sort of upright. I felt carefully up this in the dark, and came to a little square box with a knob. A light switch! I could have all the light I wanted now.

But it might give me away to the pilot if I switched it on. I left it alone, but it was a comfort to know it was there. I squatted down in the dark and pulled out my bag of food.

Cold cooked sausages, and they felt as if they were covered with chocolate biscuit crumbs. My stomach said no. I wasn't that hungry. But this was an orange. All I had to quench my thirst between here and India. I picked the skin off with my nails and tried to put the bits back into the bag. They might give me away if I left them about. I told myself I would eat half the orange and save the other half for later. I put the segments into my mouth, one by one, and savoured the juice in my dry mouth. Somehow, in the dark, I lost count and finished the lot. Perhaps we were nearly there, anyhow, I told myself.

I felt better, and got up to explore the hold further. I felt up and down the upright that I had discovered. It went up, and over, and down again the other side. It was the door frame. And that must be the handle. Ooops – I mustn't touch that! If I opened that door I might fall thousands of feet through the air on to that unknown land or sea below us.

The thought made my legs go weak. I squatted down against the side wall, away from the door, and my two voices came back.

That door! We were crazy to think we could get through it.

But we did, didn't we?

Only because somebody left it open.

Wasn't that a bit of luck?

But who left it open?

The people who brought the mail-bags. Postmen, I suppose.

It was that figure I saw on the wing. It rowed away in the dark.

You imagined it. The others didn't see it.

The dog barked. It was the gentleman, the fitter, Weber, the spy!

Mr Woods said he had gone.

He needn't have gone far. He kept keys and things to get back on board.

But we frightened him away.

He could have had time to – to put a time bomb on board.

Nothing's gone off yet.

He might have loosened some nuts or something. We may be falling apart.

Then you'd better tell the pilot.

But the pilot would bring the plane down and chuck me out.

Don't, then. But stop worrying!

I can't help worrying. I'm cold.

Get back into the sack, then. It's warmer.

I clambered back on top of the heap and searched around in the dark for the opened sack. Getting back into it took a lot longer than getting out. But I had plenty of time.

I found it, wriggled into it feet first, and curled up into a ball again. I think I must have gone off into a sort of frozen trance, like a hibernating animal with all the winter to sleep through. I had no idea how the time was passing.

I was very uncomfortable when I came to again. My voices were arguing as usual.

Aren't we over India yet?

Let's hope so.

What will they do to me when we come down?

Put you in a letterbox!

But I can't stay in this bag any longer. I'm – uncomfortable.

You shouldn't have drunk that water in Barbara's kitchen. And that was a juicy orange.

But I was thirsty.

Shouldn't pour it in if you can't pour it out.
I'll have to do it in the bag.
Over the Royal Mail? Disgusting!
Then I'll open the door and do it.
You're crazy!
I'm desperate. What shall I do?
You'll have to tell the pilot now.
But he'll bring down the plane and chuck me out.
Not if we're nearly there.

I struggled out of the sack and crawled around in the dark, looking for that light switch. Nothing to lose now. I groped along the wall, found the door frame and the knob. I turned it on – and had to screw up my eyes and rub them in the sudden dazzling light.

But there was no comfort in Mercury's hold, even though I could see it. A metal tunnel, half full of mailbags. Hadn't someone left a bucket around, or an empty paint drum? Nothing of the sort.

At the far end a ladder went up to a door. That must be the way to the flight deck. I walked stiff-legged across the gently swaying floor, climbed the ladder and tried the door. It opened.

The cramped compartment I had flown in, now lit by many little dim lights. Two figures in flying suits. One was bent over the navigator's desk. The other sat at the flight controls. Beyond his head the perspex screen was black. *Still* night-time? No, it couldn't be the same night. I had missed one whole daytime, at least. No wonder I was desperate.

The navigator was talking to himself – no, he must have been talking to the radio.

'George Able Don How Jig calling – George Able Don How Jig calling –'

At least, that was what it sounded like. But I couldn't wait. I plucked at his sleeve and made my urgent request.

His shocked face turned towards me. Staring eyes, in the face of a total stranger. His voice muttered to the intercom.

'Harold! *Harold! Navigator to pilot!*'

'What is it?' I heard Harold's faint voice. 'Have you raised Malta yet?'

A third faint voice came in. It must have been the radio. The navigator babbled.

'Those gremlins you told me about. There's a life-sized one here. It wants to be excused.'

10

Anywhere there's Water

'It wasn't Barbara's fault, sir.'

Harold was interrogating me at the navigator's desk, and the other pilot was at the controls.

'You don't have to worry about that girl. Barbara can look after herself, perfectly well,' said Harold. 'But what are we going to do with you now? That's the question.'

I had used the cramped toilet arrangement on the flight deck and was feeling better. The Malta radio station had been told to ignore the message about gremlins. I was dismayed that we hadn't got further than Malta. I hadn't held out in that hold as long as I thought. But at least they hadn't come down at Malta and chucked me out.

The co-pilot's voice came over the intercom.

'We could put him down at Cyprus. The R A F could fly him back.'

'Yes, Reggie,' Harold replied. 'And bang goes our nonstop record. And then how do we get airborne again, without Maia? We might as well go home.'

No, Harold was not pleased to see me.

'We can't take him all the way, old boy,' came the voice of Reggie. 'The police will be searching for him and his people will be worried.'

'Sir, I have no one to worry about me,' I said. I thought I would play it as pathetically as possible. 'I want to go to India.'

'Listen. This is a dangerous flight. At best it will be very, very boring. We have no room for a passenger.'

'Sir, I will not take up much room,' I said. 'I will help you – with the navigation, perhaps.'

It made him laugh. Laughter was never far away when Harold was around. He spoke on the intercom to Reggie.

'We'll keep on course for Cyprus. And we've got an assistant navigator, as far as that anyway.'

'There's the sun!' came Reggie's voice. We looked forward. There it was, struggling up over a bank of cloud, though the Mediterranean sea was still dark beneath us. 'What about a spot of breakfast now?' Reggie was asking.

'I have brought my own food,' I told Harold. I pulled from my overcoat pocket a soggy brown paper bag with five squashed sausages stuck with biscuit crumbs, and a lot of orange peel. Harold wrinkled up his nose at my offering.

'I hope we can do better than that. Go and see what's in that locker over there.'

I hurried to make myself useful. I found grapefruit juice, a vacuum jug of coffee, hardboiled eggs, split rolls, pots of butter and special marmalade. There were new enamel plates and mugs, and crisp white napkins. I spread one of these on the chart table for Harold.

I hadn't felt very hungry back in the dark hold there. But now, all this appetizing food reminded me that I hadn't really eaten for thirty-six hours. I poured coffee for Harold. The aircraft wobbled a bit.

'Hold the kite still, driver!' Harold said. 'First sitting for breakfast. Do you want yours now?'

Reggie told Harold to have his first, but to hurry up. I looked at my crumby sausages.

'When did you last eat?' Harold asked me.

I said, 'Sunday, except for an orange.'

'My God, boy! Get some food inside you,' Harold exclaimed. 'Throw that muck in the bin there and help yourself to what you fancy. Don't worry, they always give us bags too much provisions.'

Those rolls and hardboiled eggs and marmalade made the best breakfast I've ever eaten. Then I got some breakfast out for Reggie, and he handed over the controls to Harold.

'That's the cloud over Greece that Malta was trying to warn us about, once they'd stopped puzzling over our gremlin,' Reggie said to Harold. 'We can go below it, I suppose. But the mountains on Crete are over eight thousand. We don't want to prang them.'

I stole a look at the chart they had out. Quite a lot of empty white space to the west of it. That must be the sea we were crossing, now beginning to light up in the sunshine. Then a lot of jagged specks, some tiny, some long and bony. Long fingers reaching down from the north, and a lot of names in a language that must be Greek.

'Right, hold on to your coffee!' came Harold's voice. 'Losing height a bit.'

Wisps of cloud streaked past the window. Then we were under it. Ahead to the right, jagged mountains. Ahead to the left, more jagged mountains. Reggie took from the chart shelf a little book. It didn't seem to have anything to do with navigation.

'Ah, that's what I've been waiting for,' Reggie said. 'See that mountain to the north-east? That's Cyllene, or Killini.'

'What's special about it?' Harold asked.

'Hermes was born in a cave there.'

'Who's he?'

'Oh, come on, old boy! Hermes – Greek name for Mercury. Father was Zeus, King of the gods. Mother was Maia. Hermes became messenger to the gods, and his special task was to conduct the souls of the dead to the underworld.'

'Thanks!' Harold interrupted. 'Now tell us something cheerful.'

'The day he was born he turned cattle-rustler, and stole twelve cows and a hundred heifers from his brother Apollo.'

'I see,' said Harold's voice. 'Charming type! I think that's enough about Hermes, old boy. Not the sort of ideas to put in our stowaway's head.'

'Krishna stole the milkmaids' clothes when they were bathing naked. He is Indian god,' I said. I thought that might interest Reggie too, but he seemed quite shocked to hear me say it.

'Do you worship gods like that?' he asked.

'I don't, but my Indian friends do. Do you worship Hermes?'

'Of course not!'

'Then why do you read about him?'

'It's – well – it's part of your education, isn't it?'

The aircraft began to bounce around in the air quite a lot. Reggie helped me put away the breakfast things in the special racks. Then he found me a spare helmet with earphones and a microphone, strapped me into the co-pilot's seat and himself into the navigator's.

'You and your myths!' Harold grinned, battling with the controls. 'The old bus is getting ideas!'

'Always a bit dicey round Greece,' Reggie said. 'But there'll be some more open sea before Cyprus.'

Crete was to our right, a long thin brown bony island, just like the map of it.

'We can't get a weather report out of Crete, can we?' Harold asked.

'Not one of our places, old chap,' Reggie told him.

'Why isn't it?' Harold sounded quite peeved.

'We don't really need Crete,' said Reggie. 'We've got Gibraltar at one end of the Med, Malta in the middle, and Cyprus the other end. Who needs Crete? The Greeks can keep it.'

I said, 'Lucky old Greeks!' But I suppose I shouldn't have done.

'What's lucky about not belonging to the Empire?' Harold demanded. I couldn't tell how serious he was, so I kept my mouth shut.

'Icarian Sea,' I heard Reggie say. I twisted round and saw that he was reading from his book again. 'Icarus, son of Daedalus, tried to escape from Crete by flying with feathers fixed to his arms with wax. But he imprudently flew too close to the sun, whose rays melted the wax and caused him to fall into the sea, where he drowned.'

'Oh, for God's sake put that book away, Reggie!' Harold exploded. *He* seemed to believe these stories, anyway.

The lazy surf curled very slowly round the end of Crete. Open sea stretched ahead, and Mercury settled down to level flight. The sky cleared, though far to the north I could see a cloudy and mountainous coastline. Below us the sea was clear blue, and the tiny shadow of our aircraft skimmed over the rippled surface. Now and then there was a V-shaped wake on the water, with a tiny puffing steamer or a white sail in the point of it. The many little dials on the instrument panel in front of me kept still and steady. Alongside me, the pilot seldom adjusted his controls. This was air travel – calm and untroubled, with the world at your feet! And, yes, even a bit boring.

Well fed, warm, and relaxed in my comfortable seat, I had time to think about my mission to India. I couldn't fail. I wasn't Icarus, with feathers stuck to his arms with wax. I was Hermes – or Mercury, or whatever I liked to call myself – messenger of the gods and a god himself, with divine wings on his sandals. Perhaps I shouldn't think about those pagan gods, though. But angels and archangels, Michael and Gabriel, they had wings, didn't they? We were a little lower than the angels, but not much, now!

Reggie's voice interrupted my thoughts. It sounded serious.

'We're coming up to the point of no return, Harold. If we want to turn south for Port Said, Suez and the Red Sea, now's the time to decide.'

'Remind me of the pros and cons,' Harold said.

'If we go via the Red Sea we have open water beneath us all the way – that's if we count the Suez Canal. And we've got friendly bases in Egypt and Aden. But it's fifteen hundred miles further, and of course we have to save fuel. If we go to the Euphrates we've got a hundred and fifty miles of desert, not very friendly, to cross before we see water under our floats. But that's only an hour's flight, and we'll soon be over friends in Habbaniyah.'

'Our orders are to do it unless the weather's impossible?'

'That's it.'

'Call up the RAF in Cyprus then.'

Our mood of calm came to an end as we heard the radio howling and crackling. At last Reggie seemed to have succeeded, though we only heard his own voice.

'George Able Don How Jig calling Larnaca. Are you receiving me, over? . . . Yes, seaplane Mercury, pilots Singer and Thorpe, Royal Mail cargo . . .'

I held my breath and listened. *Now he would tell them about me!*

'Can you give me a weather forecast for the Syrian Desert? Over . . .'

Then he was speaking to Harold over the intercom. 'They reckon four-tenths cloud over the desert. More than an even chance of seeing where we're going. What do you think, Captain?'

'We'll do it.'

They had forgotten me!

Another long rocky coastline stretched to the south of us, with more cloudy mountains in the distance. A finger of land pointed eastwards into the sea, and we went where it pointed. Then, ahead of us, a solid mass of land loomed up.

'Here we go, chaps,' said Harold. 'Say good-bye to the Mediterranean.'

He adjusted the controls, the four engines roared at a higher pitch, the horizon sank downwards, and we were climbing over dry mountains.

'There's a railway line if you can spot it,' Reggie said.

'What time's the next train?' Harold asked, his eyes on his instruments.

I looked down. We had crossed a lush green coastal strip, then rocky gorges running down to the sea, and now we were over the crest of the mountains and above the higher land. A skinny river ran across our flight path. I pointed down excitedly.

'Sir, is that the River Jordan?'

'I'm afraid not,' said Reggie. 'But the Jordan runs down the same valley, further south. We're crossing over Jordan, in a way.'

There was the railway, and a road too, crossing the river by a flat-roofed town. There wasn't much else to see in this empty land. Stony hilltops, flat valleys with a very few villages, just clusters of little white beehives. They were joined together by a spider's web of white tracks. Here and there were signs of green crops growing, and some sort of trees planted in orchards. But no sign of open water at all now.

A bit of a smoky haze ahead. Was that a jumble of white rock beneath it? No, there in the hollow lay a large town, a city, built all of white stone. In the middle of it a grim fortress on a high mound, reaching up to us.

'Aleppo!' said Reggie. 'Do you know Shakespeare thought it was a seaport?'

'A good job he's not navigating,' Harold said. 'I don't like the look of those chaps down there.'

We could see little white dots on the roads below, which must be people. They looked all right. What was Harold worrying about?

'Not one of our places, is it?' Harold said.

'No,' said Reggie. 'The French look after it. We've got their permission to overfly.'

'I hope they've not forgotten,' Harold said. 'Look – fighters!' There was a little airfield down there with two-winged aeroplanes waiting. 'Where do we go from here?'

'Just follow those camels,' said Reggie. There ahead of us was a string of four-footed creatures, tied nose to tail, setting out into the dusty, empty landscape. 'They can go for days without water, you know.'

'That's just what worries me,' Harold said grimly. 'We've got to look for a river.'

Somehow the seat I was sitting in didn't feel so comfortable now. It wasn't like the time when we were flying happily over the Mediterranean Sea, it was more like walking over dead bones in the graveyard, with your toes curling up. Only we were flying over the dead stones of a desert, knowing that if we had to come down the landing would be very hard indeed. And now, with the heat-haze blotting out the horizon all round us, there was nothing to look at but dry earth and desolation. What was Mercury doing, a *seaplane*, in the middle of all this land?

A spectral, whirling shape came rushing over the desert towards us. Another, and a third!

'Dust devils!' said Harold, and swore. He adjusted the controls again, the engines gained power, and we were climbing over the approaching storm. Now there was nothing to look at but sky, and cloud beneath us, and even at this height Mercury was bucking and kicking in the turbulent air.

'I thought they said only four-tenths cloud,' Harold said.

'They did,' said Reggie. 'The other six-tenths must be somewhere else.'

'What happens if we overshoot the Euphrates, with this stuff below us?'

'We'll know it when we hit the Zagros Mountains. We'd better alter course on dead reckoning. I'll let you know when.'

I began to feel dizzy, and breathing seemed difficult. Harold had the mask of his helmet fixed across his mouth, and now and then he took his eyes off his instruments and looked anxiously across at me.

'We'll have to lose height,' I heard him mutter, though I wasn't really listening. 'The kid's got no oxygen. We'd no right to bring him.'

I was still looking listlessly out of the window.

'Water!' I remember how feeble my voice was.

'You can have some in a minute,' Harold said.

'No,' I said. 'Down there.' There had been a break in the clouds and I'd seen the sunlight gleaming on a bright strip far below.

'By God, he's right!' Harold exclaimed. He eased over the controls, the plane banked round and down, and circled down through more breaks in the clouds until we could see the river winding through narrow green banks across the desert.

'I suppose that is Euphrates?' Harold queried.

'Can't be anything else,' Reggie said. 'Well spotted, young feller!'

I was breathing easily again, and was pleased with myself for finding the river. But Harold still looked a bit doubtful.

'Looks all right for a spot of trout fishing, Reggie. But we can't put down on that.'

'We don't have to, do we?' Reggie said. 'And it's bound to get bigger as it goes along. It only needed a drop of extra rain to float Noah's ark.'

'Here we go again – Reggie's conducted tour!' Harold laughed. 'What about another meal? I'm peckish again.'

I found cold chicken and salad in the food locker, and Reggie and I had first go. Then the pilots changed over again. We were flying over villages now, with green culti-vated patches.

'We might try calling Habbaniyah now,' Reggie said from the controls. 'Do you want me to do it?'

'Leave it to me,' said Harold. 'I think I've got a chum down there, expecting me. Old Jimmy Mortimer. I'll see if I can raise him.'

As I cleared away the meal Harold started the monotonous call into the radio mike. It sounded nonsense. 'George Able Don How Jig calling Habbaniyah – George Able Don How Jig calling Habbaniyah . . .' In between calls the radio speaker whined and crackled, but there was no reply. Harold gave it a rest and I was able to ask him a question.

'Why don't you speak English?'

'That's English,' Harold said. 'It's our call sign. The blokes at Habbaniyah speak English all right. There's an RAF base there, just where we need it. Mess-pot.'

'I beg your pardon?' I had to say. I hadn't understood the last bit.

'Mess-pot. Mesopotamia. Ask Reggie what it means.'

'Mesopotamia?' Reggie said. 'The land between the rivers. Tigris and Euphrates. It all started there: Noah, Abraham, Nebuchadnezzar – all that lot. And now it's our turn to look after it, but I don't think our fellows have much fun there.'

Harold started calling again, and this time a faint reply came over the speaker. It was a voice rather like Harold's.

'Habbaniyah control calling George Able Don How Jig. Is that you, Harold, you old stinker? Over.'

'Hello, Jimmy! Not receiving you very clearly. Have you been drinking too much down there? Over.'

'Nothing else to do here, old boy. But why don't you come down and join us in the mess? Over?'

'Jolly decent of you to invite us, old chap, but I don't think we can stop. Over.'

Reggie's voice came over the intercom. 'Airfield in sight

ahead!' And now the chatty English voice from the ground came back loud and clear.

'Mercury ahoy! Seeing you bright and clear. I say, Harold, old boy, I've got bad news for you! Over.'

'What's that, Jimmy? Suddenly run out of beer? Over.'

'You've got no undercart, old chap. Your wheels have fallen off!' And we heard a guffaw of jolly laughter before the 'Over'.

Harold replied, 'I was aware of that, old man. That's why we can't stop. Over.'

'Try coming down on our duck pond. I'll get the ducks to move over. Over.'

'Thanks very much, but I think we'll push on. I've got a date in Calcutta.'

My own ears pricked up at that, underneath the headphones. Calcutta? So that was where we were going. I hadn't even asked.

The jokey voice from the land of Nebuchadnezzar was running on. 'You need to watch out for these oriental beauties, young Harold. Do you know the story about the missionary and the nautch girl? Over.'

'Jimmy, *please!* We've got children listening here. Over.' I saw Harold bite his lips as he realized what he said.

'You've got *what?* Over.'

'Er – it's the co-pilot. Young Reggie. You know, he's a bit prim and proper. Look, Jimmy, what's the weather like down there? Over.'

'Bloody hot, as usual. Hang on, the met officer says there's something on the way . . .' *Crackle, crackle! Wheeooow* . . . The voice had faded away. Harold began to call and call again. But Habbaniyah airfield was now behind us and we heard no more from them.

'Silly ass!' Harold fumed. 'I should have known better than to try to get sense out of Jimmy Mortimer. Never mind. Push on, Reggie, the weather looks settled enough.'

On the ground below us the shadows of palm trees grew longer. Behind our right-hand wing the sun was nearing the horizon. Yet we hadn't had lunch long ago. Why was this? I asked Reggie.

'Tuesday night is rushing to meet us at over a thousand miles an hour,' Reggie said. 'And we're flying to meet it at a hundred and fifty. So our day's short, by about three hours. One day perhaps we'll get a machine to hang in the sky at over a thousand miles an hour, and it will always be tea-time.'

Well, that gave me something to think about, though the last bit must have been a joke, mustn't it?

Harold said to Reggie, 'If you're happy cruising down the river, I'll get a bit of shut-eye.'

'Okay, old boy,' said Reggie. 'You didn't get much over France last night.'

Harold tilted back the co-pilot's seat comfortably, and we had to be quiet so as not to disturb him.

Quiet? Now there was no chat, the thunder of the Napier engines seemed louder than ever, and I began to think about them again. We had flown for a night and a day – we must be about half-way now – how much longer could they keep thundering? I settled down in the navigator's seat and looked at the books and papers in the tidy rack. I wasn't sleepy. I had slept more than enough the day before.

Myths of Ancient Greece and the Middle East – that was the book Reggie was getting his stories out of. But I wanted maths, not myths.

Manual of Air Navigation, that was more like it. I

opened it and looked at pages of figures. More interesting than leaky bath-tubs in *Godfrey and Price*. Yet perhaps sums about taps and plug-holes weren't so useless. They had poured all that petrol into the tanks at Rochester, and now it was pouring out into the engines. Where did they keep it all?

Short Seaplane 'Mercury': Specifications, a neatly bound folder of typed pages. *Fuel system*. Here it was. So they stowed a lot of the petrol in those big floats down there! I was glad I didn't know that when we were crossing the rocky desert. Even now it gave me an uncomfortable feeling, like walking over grave-stones. If we had come down on the rocks with floats full of petrol? WHOOOSH! A petrol explosion as soon as we touched!

I stole a look through the observation window. There was no direct sunlight on the river below, but I could see it clearly and it looked comfortably wider. I turned back to the booklet.

Fuel capacity . . . Fuel consumption . . . Fuel gauges . . . It was all there. I began to do sums on the navigator's pad. Wait a minute, what was this? Something in the drawer in a long thin case. A *slide rule*. Only the most senior boys were allowed to use them at school, but somebody had shown me. You slid the wooden slide out and read off the measurements, and it did your multiplying and dividing for you. Well, would it tell me how much petrol we had used and how much we'd got left?

Anyway, this was better than lying in the dark as I'd done the night before, with nothing to do but *worry*.

There were charts laid out ready, too, with pencilled lines for the course we were supposed to fly on, and there were silvery dividers with sharp points to measure off distances. As I worked on, the flight deck grew dark, and I switched on a shaded lamp. I laughed to myself at what I saw on my pad – those Indian figures that so annoyed Mr Percival, they had crept back into my calculations. Never mind, Indian figures would get me back to India.

But when I got a final answer I didn't like it much. I went all over my workings again but it still came out the same. I thought I'd better tell Reggie.

Our flight was now very smooth and level, and the pilot seemed to have nothing to do. I went quietly forward to the controls and touched Reggie's arm. He jumped, as he had done the first time I touched him.

'I calculate we'll run out of petrol over English Gunge,' I told him.

He smiled and looked down at the pad I was holding. He looked at all the figures.

'Did you do all that?' he asked.

'Yes, sir,' I said.

'It has kept you out of mischief, hasn't it?'

He looked closely at some gauges.

'I shouldn't worry, though. We're half-way there and the gauges show plenty in reserve. Why don't you get some sleep?'

I looked at the gauges too. Either I was wrong, or they were.

'It's plain sailing tonight at least,' said Reggie. 'Look, that's the Persian Gulf.'

The rising moon was making a golden path over the sea.

Over the Viceroy's Head

I had been used to sleeping on the floor in India.

I slept right through that second night on board Mercury, though I was half aware of the pilots stepping over me from time to time. I woke feeling quite fresh. But an awful thought struck me. We hadn't crossed above India while I slept, had we? I hadn't missed my homecoming?

The pilots – they hadn't slept so well – were edgy with each other. Harold was at the controls. The flight deck was beginning to get light.

'Where are we?' he asked Reggie sharply.

'Don't know,' said Reggie, poring over the chart.

'What d'you mean, you don't know? You're the navigator, aren't you?'

Reggie replied calmly, 'Well, we are flying along latitude 25 degrees north, that I do know. We've kept the coast of Persia to port all night. So out there that's either Persia or India.'

'*Is it India?*' I sprang up from the floor and looked out.

All I could see was a dark and desolate coast with wild mountains rising from it. We were flying along it, over the sea.

'I shouldn't think they care, down there,' said Reggie. 'Do you want to find out?'

Of course I did! He spoke as if it didn't *matter!*

He took his time opening a polished wooden box and taking out a brass instrument, like the ones you see pictures of old sea-captains using. He cleaned its little lens carefully with a bit of soft leather.

'We'll take a dawn sight, as soon as the sun's clear of the horizon. Can you use a stop-watch?'

I nodded eagerly. If only he would hurry up!

He gave me an ordinary stop-watch like the ones they used for sports at school. We looked ahead at the sun beginning to peep up over the sea. Soon it was too bright to look at. Reggie screwed a dark glass over the lens. He held the sextant to his eye.

'*Now!*'

I pressed the knob of the stop-watch. I read off the minutes and seconds; he looked at the chronometer on the wall and noted down figures. I found in my pocket the paper and pencil that Mouse had given me and began my own calculations.

Reggie glanced over at what I was doing, and was amazed.

'How did you learn to do that?'

'Out of the book, last night,' I told him. 'The dawn sight's the easy one, isn't it?'

'Good God!' Reggie muttered. 'Hey, Harold, this kid's doing my sums for me!'

'Fine!' Harold replied, still sounding cross. 'Perhaps he'll tell me where we are.'

Reggie and I both scribbled calculations. I don't say we

were racing. I wanted to be first to say we were over India. It didn't matter to him. He let me use the dividers to measure the longitude over the chart.

I jumped up and looked out at the coast. *Yes*, there was a bay and a headland just where they ought to be. The cape on the chart had a name: *Ras Pishkan*. I had never heard of it, but the chart showed the Indian border to the west.

'*That is India!*' I announced, pointing.

'Good oh!' said Harold. 'I didn't think we could miss it.'

I knew I was still fifteen hundred miles from my own home. But India was my country. Hundreds of millions of people lived there, speaking hundreds of different languages. The chart said that was Baluchistan I was looking at. Had I ever met anyone from Baluchistan? I think I did once, and I didn't like him. Never mind, India was the mother of all of us. In a way, I was home already!

Of course it didn't mean the same for Harold and Reggie. They were beginning to show the strain of the long flight, and there was weariness in their voices.

'It's still more than two hours' flying time to Karachi,' Reggie said. 'Time for a shave and breakfast.'

'Shall we chuck it in, Reggie, old boy? Go down at Karachi? Have a shower, change of clothes, a drink and a decent lunch? I know a good hotel there, and there's an excellent club.'

Harold was stretching his tense arms in the pilot's seat.

'Very tempting, Harold,' said Reggie. 'I almost wish you meant it.'

I hoped he didn't. Karachi meant nothing to me, and I didn't see myself fitting in at those posh hotels and clubs. Yes, India was my country, but people like Harold and Reggie had the best of it.

'I wish I meant it too,' Harold said. 'But it's Calcutta or bust. Can we make it in daylight?'

'At our best cruising speed we've got the time. But have we got the fuel?'

'Don't ask me, tell me.'

'I'll tell you something funny. Murugan did his sums last night and said we'd run out of fuel over – where was it?'

'English Gunge,' I reminded him. They both laughed.

'If we must come down in the gunge it might as well be English,' Harold said. 'But just check those figures will you, Reggie?'

I got them their breakfast, opening a tin of sardines. As Harold ate, I looked down at the sea through the observation window. The sunlit ripples were far below, but I could clearly see shadowy shapes beneath them.

'Big fish!' I said.

'Sharks,' said Harold.

I shuddered.

'I do not like sharks,' I said.

'Some people don't,' said Harold. 'I can't stand snakes.'

After his breakfast Reggie consulted the fuel gauges again, looked a little puzzled, and did some calculations on the slide rule. He seemed to be doing much the same sort of sums as I had done myself.

'It's okay, Skipper,' he announced. 'Fuel consumption seems to be surprisingly low. We should make Calcutta by daylight, with something in hand. And there had better be a *very* good club in Calcutta.'

Karachi came in sight, with its bay and port full of steamers and liners, and its sprawling, smoking city. Harold changed places with Reggie again to speak to someone on the radio. We came down lower and circled above the airfield. Little figures waved, and the voice over the radio came loud and clear. But there was no joking and chaff this time. The English voice was firm and confident.

'. . . three hours' flying up the course of the Indus and Sutlej rivers. For the first two hours anyway, you've got plenty of water to come down on if you're in trouble. Then the Yamuna's within an hour's flying, but you're on your own over the plains there. Say hello to the Viceroy over New Delhi – yes, they'll be looking out for you – then you've got the company of the Yamuna or the Ganges itself for another five hours. Plenty of deep water. The weather's clear over Western India, but I'm afraid there's a chance of early monsoon clouds over Bengal. They've got floods there – but that shouldn't worry you, should it! I'll telegraph Calcutta to expect you. Good luck and happy landing! Over and out!'

We flew off, gaining height again. No difficulty in finding the mighty river, snaking away to the north between its green banks, until it faded into the heat haze of the horizon.

'That is *Indus!*' I said to Harold, hardly able to speak for awe.

'Big, isn't it,' he replied casually.

'It is one of the *sacred* rivers of India,' I said. 'I do not think many Indians have seen it as I am seeing it.'

'Probably not,' he said.

'I feel I am the god Vishnu, flying on the sacred bird Garuda!'

He looked at me oddly.

'You didn't learn that in Rochester cathedral,' he commented. I felt a bit embarrassed. He was right – but this was *India*.

'Aircraft in sight!' Reggie reported. Then, 'No, it isn't. It's a damn bird.'

I could see it clearly below us, wheeling calmly on its great broad wings. That was the way to fly, silently, without the roar of engines, with nothing to obstruct your view of the broad world beneath you.

'Is that your sacred bird?' Harold asked.

'No, that is vulture. He is looking for a dead cow, or a dead Parsee,' I told him.

The morning hours wore on, and the pilots hardly altered the controls, and still the great Indus was below us.

'Aircraft in sight!' Reggie reported again. 'It really is, this time. Unless it's a flying dustbin.'

Harold and I looked out. There it was, ahead and to one side of us. We were very rapidly overtaking it.

'Aaah!' Harold sighed. 'Mr Thorpe, you are speaking of the aeroplane I love! Don't be rude to the woppity!'

Its top and bottom wings seemed to be tied to the body with strings. The naked engine was stuck on in front, with its exhaust pipe trailing downwards. Its wheels were on the end of stumpy legs, and the head of the pilot and the gunner, and one machine gun, stuck out of the top. We could see the men waving their gloved hands.

'Give the woppity a waggle, Reggie. They won't be able to keep up with us,' said Harold. The horizon seesawed as Reggie waggled our wings.

'Why do you call it a woppity, sir?' I had to ask.

'That's what it is,' Harold said. 'W-A-P-I-T-I. I used to fly them, to drop bombs on the faker of Ippy.'

What was he talking about? Then I remembered.

'The Faquir of Ipi, sir? My brother told me he was a Freedom Fighter –' I could have bitten my tongue off. That was *not* the right thing to say.

'I'd call him a bloody old terrorist,' Harold scowled. 'What side's your brother on?'

Coming home had made me careless. Luckily Reggie interrupted.

'Do we go left or right?'

Ahead and below the river forked. Really of course one river flowed into another. We were flying upstream.

'Keep right, and right again at the next junction,' Harold said.

The pilots changed places again and Reggie came and looked at the chart with me.

'One two three four five rivers,' he counted.

'*Panch ab*,' I said.

'What's that?'

'You say Punjab,' I told him. 'It is the land of the five rivers. Jhelum, Chenab, Ravi, Beas and Sutlej. I will tell you something about the Beas. Your great King Alexander came from Europe, and stopped there.'

'He wept because he had no more worlds to conquer,' Reggie said. 'That's what we learned at school.'

'He did not even conquer India,' I said. 'He went home from here.'

'He was only a Greek,' said Reggie. 'The British got a bit further.'

Then they will have further to go home. No, I didn't say it out loud.

'Poor old Alexander,' Harold's voice came over the intercom. 'He had to walk, and it's tedious enough flying. India does go on and on.'

Yes, you need patience to travel over India, whether you go on foot, by ox-cart, by train or in an aeroplane. Down below, the River Sutlej became ever narrower and stonier. I could see flat stretches where the riverside rocks were spread with brightly coloured patches, and I knew it was where the women came to wash their clothes and put them out to dry.

'No point in sticking to this river, Reggie,' Harold said. 'What about cutting across to the Yamuna? Can you give us a course?'

'Okay, Harold. Let's just pinpoint a position. Right, course one zero zero.'

We banked round to the east and climbed to gain height above the plateau. I had seen little jagged white clouds far ahead, but now I gasped. Not clouds – mountain tops. Snow-covered peaks!

'Himalayas!'

'What are you talking about?' Reggie muttered from the navigating table. 'They should be two hundred miles away.'

Then he looked, and gasped too. He checked the chart, but decided they *were* two hundred miles away. Yet they were sharp in the clear air, peak after white peak, like a frieze painted along the bottom of the sky. And they stayed on our left hand as we flew across the flat plain. Almost directly below us the tiny shadow of our aircraft flitted over squares of standing crops, and over a criss-cross of little canals and streams.

'Don't try to put down on any of those ditches, Harold,' Reggie advised.

'We don't need to, do we?' Harold's voice came back. 'Those engines have kept going since Monday. We can't miss the Yamuna, can we?'

'Difficult to miss all five hundred miles of it, old boy – and a thousand miles of Ganges as a second choice.'

They changed places again and Harold started fiddling with the radio. Almost immediately a strong signal came back and Harold reached for the message pad and pencil. He started writing down what the toneless English voice on the radio was saying at dictation speed.

We have pleasure – in congratulating – Imperial Airways –comma – the design team – of Short Brothers –comma – and the pilots – of the seaplane Mercury – on the great achievement – of their nonstop flight – from England to New Delhi – stop – this event – is of the utmost significance – in the development – of communications – within our great Empire –stop – We wish pilots Singer and Thorpe – all success – in their onward flight – to Calcutta – stop – signed Linlithgow.

'Whew!' Harold whistled, mopping his forehead. He read the wordy message back to the radio station to check it, then he had to read it all out again to Reggie on the intercom.

'What d'you make of that, Reggie? And we're not even at Delhi yet. Keep your fingers crossed.'

'Who do you say signed it?' Reggie's voice asked.

'Only the *Viceroy*, old chap! You know, King George has to put up with old ruins like Windsor Castle. But the Viceroy of India has got the world's newest palace, and a dozen rajahs to polish his boots.'

I didn't think it was true about the rajahs. But something came back to me. *What could I do – I, Murugan, who blacks the prefect's shoes?* And an insane plan started forming in my head.

'Suppose we ought to send him back a signal in the same sort of lingo,' Harold said. 'I'm hopeless at this high-falutin' stuff. Would you like to do it, Reggie?'

'I'd rather be checking things for the last leg of the flight,' Reggie said.

Was this my chance? Could my plan really work?

'I will write your message,' I said quietly.

Harold goggled at me. Then he laughed.

'Good God – you'd probably do it better than us! Have a go!'

And he handed me the pad and pencil. The pilots had other things to think about.

'Yamuna's ahead!' Reggie announced. No, we could hardly miss it. Broad and glistening, it ran from north to south across our flight path. Reggie banked round to the right, and now we were flying above it – a comforting feeling, to have deep water under our floats again.

Harold was still talking over the radio. He ceased, and turned off the transmission switch.

'We're invited to fly over the Viceroy's palace, chaps! I've promised not to drop anything. His Excellency may even lean out of the window and wave.'

'We're honoured!' said Reggie. 'But where the hell is it? I didn't bring a street map.'

'I dare say I could find it,' Harold told him. 'The streets are all straight lines. I've been along them in a rickshaw.'

He joined Reggie in one of the forward seats. I listened to their talk as I sat in the navigator's seat and craned my neck at the observation window to look at the capital city of India, which I had never seen. The plane lost height.

Harold said, 'There's the Jamuna Bridge, and the Red Fort.'

And there was the smoke, and the jumble of old houses, mosques and temples, and the great red fortress. That must be Old Delhi, and then New Delhi was below us with its broad highways radiating from a great archway. Gardens with flowering trees. Motor-cars, buses, pony-carts and bicycles. As we came down lower, people stopped to point up at us, and wave. A vast brick building with white columns.

'The palace,' said Harold.

Soldiers in coloured turbans. Men in black suits standing

on the broad steps. The whole scene seesawed as Harold waggled Mercury's wings.

'I hope we gave him time to put his pre-lunch drink down,' Harold said – and below us the scene rapidly changed to poor, dusty suburbs.

We banked over the airfield, where uniformed figures alongside Royal Air Force planes waved enthusiastically. And then we were climbing, and heading back over the great river, where we belonged.

'And I hope we didn't waste too much fuel on that jaunt,' said Reggie, glancing at the fuel gauges again. 'Never mind, it made a break.'

'We'd better reply to that signal before we get out of radio touch,' Harold said. 'How's the message coming on, Murugan?'

I was just pencilling in the last words. I got up from the navigator's seat and handed the paper to Harold, who read it out to Reggie.

ON BEHALF OF IMPERIAL AIRWAYS AND THE LOYAL WORKERS OF SHORT BROTHERS, THE PILOTS OF SEAPLANE MERCURY HUMBLY BEG TO SEND GREETINGS FROM ON HIGH TO HIS EXCELLENCY THE VICEROY OF INDIA, WITH HEARTFELT THANKS FOR HIS ESTEEMED AND AUSPICIOUS WISHES FOR OUR ONWARD JOURNEY, WHICH CANNOT FAIL TO ENSURE ITS UTTER SUCCESS. SHANMUGAM AZAD KARO.

Reggie exploded into laughter. 'We can't send that stuff! He'll think we're pulling his leg!'

I said, 'But that is how we say things in India. His Excellency will expect it.'

'He's right, you know,' Harold came to my rescue. 'As I

said, India goes on and on. But what's that last bit, Murugan?'

'Oh, in India we always end messages with those words. They bring good luck,' I told him. And I kept my fingers crossed, a trick I had learned at King's School.

'You wouldn't like to read it all over the radio, would you, Murugan?' Harold asked me, concentrating on adjustments to the controls.

'He can't,' said Reggie. 'He's still not officially with us, is he?'

'Good God, I suppose not,' Harold said. 'He'll have to face the music in Calcutta.'

I made way for him at the radio. I heard him read my whole message at dictation speed. I thought he was going to miss out the three Indian words, but he spelt them into the microphone, letter by letter.

'I don't suppose the Viceroy's listening,' he said when he'd finished. 'But it's all on a Secretariat file now.'

It had worked! I would never get closer to the Viceroy of India than where we were now, three thousand feet above his head. But I'd got my three-word message through! I'd have to face the music in Calcutta, but I didn't mind. I had done my family duty.

Calcutta was still six hundred miles away. We had all the afternoon to fly through yet.

'Next stop Agra,' Reggie said, as we levelled out over the river. 'Did you ever see the Taj Mahal, Harold?'

'That is the most beautiful building in the world,' I thought I ought to tell them.

'So they say,' said Harold. 'No, I never got round to it.'

'You're supposed to see it by moonlight,' Reggie said. But Harold said we couldn't wait that long. I got them some lunch in the forty minutes we took to fly to Agra.

We were flying high now, and the afternoon heat haze obscured the land beneath us.

'Do you think that's it?' Reggie asked as we peered down over a bend in the river.

'Looks like a boiled egg on a tray,' said Harold. We flew on. I dozed in the afternoon. So did Harold. It is not shameful to sleep in the afternoon, in India. I must have had quite a long sleep before Reggie's voice woke me up.

'Something odd going on down there! The river bank's on fire and all the people are in the water! Do you think we ought to help?'

I rubbed my eyes and looked down. Below us the river was broader than ever, and what Reggie said seemed to be true. Then I guessed where we were.

'I do not think those people need our help,' I told him. 'Those are all Hindus. On the banks they are burning the dead bodies. In the water they are washing away their sins. That must be Varanasi – or, as you say, Benares. And that is Ganga, Ganges, the holiest of all rivers!'

After a short silence Reggie said, 'My aunt had a brass tray from Benares.' We flew on. More and more of the land below became bright green. I knew what that colour must mean. Paddy fields. Rice. And great stretches were covered with brown water.

'Plenty of water down there now,' Reggie said.

'Let's hope we don't need it,' said Harold. 'Look what's coming up ahead.'

I looked ahead. Snow-mountains? No. Clouds.

I couldn't help exclaiming, 'Oh, how beautiful!'

The sun was moving down the sky behind us. It shone on the banks and peaks of the clouds that were billowing up in front of us, thousands of feet high. Only their undersides looked dark and dirty. And down there bright light flickered too. Lightning!

Harold and Reggie didn't seem to find the clouds beautiful. They seemed to become different people, no longer wasting words or wasting time. Harold was captain of the aircraft now.

'Reggie, what's the flying time to our destination?'

'Two hours at cruising speed.'

'Have we got fuel for increased speed?'

'According to the gauges, yes, but –'

'But what?'

'Yes, we must have.'

'Take the co-pilot's seat. I'll need you on the instruments. And, Murugan, strap yourself into the navigator's seat and stay there.'

We both did as he ordered.

'We'll have to go under it,' Harold said. The plane's nose dipped and we dived for the dark underside of the clouds. The engines roared at a higher pitch. Wisps of cloud passed by us. The whole great mass of vapour seemed to glow like an electric light bulb as the lightning passed through it. We were down there in the gloom, rain lashing the windows, the plane bucketing and swaying as the two pilots worked on the controls. Another flash of lightning lit up the cabin, and a shattering clap of thunder shook us, above the noise of the engines.

Yes, I was very frightened. This was my punishment for thinking I was a god or an angel, coming to set the world to rights. The gods always punished such pride. I couldn't help thinking it was one of the Indian gods who ruled this storm, Indra, ancient god of the thunder. But I could not pray to a heathen god. The words I ought to use came into my mind:

> *. . . we have followed too much the devices and desires of our own hearts, we have offended against Thy holy laws, we have left undone those things which we ought to have done . . .*

Something left undone. It had been nagging my mind ever since I first spoke to the pilots. Something I should have told them. But what was it? The plane seemed to fall into a pit, then fetched up with a jolt that left the wings shaking. But it had jolted my memory.

'Captain, sir?' I said weakly into the intercom. 'I beg permission to speak.'

'What is it?' Harold snapped. 'It had better be important.'

'Sir, I told lies about how I got on board to stow away. Barbara and William rowed me in a boat and –'

'Forget it!' Harold interrupted. 'I've got other things to think about.'

'But, sir, I thought I saw – I'm *sure* I saw someone else rowing away from the planes–' A gust of wind lifted Mercury and shook it viciously. Harold wrestled with the controls.

'Look, it doesn't *matter!*' he growled between his teeth. But I had to tell him.

'*I think it was Weber and I think he sabotaged the fuel gauges,*' I got out.

'My God!' Harold swore. 'Why didn't you tell me before? Reggie, how much fuel *have* we got left?'

Reggie's voice came in. 'If those gauges are telling lies – very little, perhaps. We may have to ditch. But look at those floods!'

Ahead of us the whole country was under water. Mile upon mile of water churned by the rain, with mop-headed palm trees sticking up and tormented by the wind. We flew over little islands of huts, roofed with palm-leaf thatch. They were not far beneath the floats of the plane now, and we could see the cattle huddled between the huts, on the low mounds that stood above the flood water.

'Hell! Where's the river gone?' Harold cursed. There was no direction in this watery scene, no clear river banks, no sun, no roads or railways. Even the wind seemed to come from all directions at once.

'Fly due south,' Reggie said. 'We can't miss the Bay of Bengal.'

'Can't we? How do you tell land from sea here?' Harold asked.

One of the engines coughed, spluttered, picked up again.

I think we all froze in our seats. Those engines had roared above our heads for thousands of miles, ever since Monday. If they went sick now, it seemed the end of everything.

The engine spluttered again. Harold leant forward to the control panel and turned a switch. The engine died. Before the other three engines could skew the plane round, Harold turned another switch, and an engine died on the other side.

'We'll make Calcutta on two engines,' Harold said quietly. 'And save fuel.' But I could see his helmeted head looking from side to side over the waters – looking for somewhere to come down if we had to.

I craned my neck to look too. At least I had seen floods in India. I thought I could tell the difference between a paddyfield and a river.

'Look to the right, sir. Boats!'

'No time to look at boats, boy!' Harold growled.

'But it must be the river!' I insisted.

He must have seen what I meant. He banked round. As he did so, another engine cut out. Harold cursed, and switched off the last one.

Silence! The roar we had lived with for nearly two days – it was gone. Well, not quite silence. Now we could hear the rush of the air over the skin of the aircraft, and its eerie whine through the struts of the floats. Everything depended on those floats now. I was so glad they weren't wheels.

Harold put the nose down. The surface of the water came up to meet us.

'Not there! Not there!' I shouted. 'That is paddyfield! Shallow water! Go further on!' I could see the pattern of the planted rice under the water. I didn't know how much water Mercury needed, but I thought it should be deeper than a rice stalk!

Harold managed to lift the plane out of its downward glide for a moment. Then down we came again, towards flowing, turbulent water.

It was a slow, heavy touch-down. Spray showered upwards. We pitched like a rocking-horse as we moved on over the water. Out of a rain squall ahead loomed a brick-red tower, set with gods, demons, dancing figures.

'Mind the temple!' I shouted. 'Stop!'

There were no brakes or anything to stop us. But a giant hand seemed to grab the floats from beneath. We all pitched forward against our seat-belts. Navigation instruments and enamel mugs came crashing to the floor of the flight deck. Mercury's nose ducked downwards towards the muddy water – we were going to turn floats-over-engines!

No, we weren't. Everything came to a stop. Mercury settled back again, more or less level.

It was very quiet. We had arrived in India.

12

Freedom Fighters

It was morning.

We had spent the night in the silent plane. And in darkness, too. The darkness of the storm had passed into the darkness of night. Harold and Reggie, after trying in vain to get the radio going, had stretched out on the floor wherever they could, to catch up with the sleep they had missed over the last two days.

I had sat for a while at the open door of the hold, staring out at the damp darkness that was India, wondering why my mother country was so *uncomfortable*. And then I remembered. I was still wearing two woolly vests and two pairs of woolly pants, plus pyjama trousers, all under my ordinary jacket and trousers. I had forgotten that India was hot. I stripped off until I was comfortable, and sat and looked at the darkness and listened to the silence.

I had been living with the thunder of the engines for so long that I thought my ears were still ringing. But no, the sound came from the darkness, like hundreds of little engines beating time together. Frogs! But it was a gentle, sleepy sound. I made up a bed for myself on discarded clothes and slept peacefully until dawn, lulled by frogs and water noises.

And now the sun was shining and the sky was clear, and the floodwaters were steaming in the morning heat. Harold and Reggie had given up looking like pilots in their flying-suits and stripped down to something comfortable too. Just two men showing rather a lot of pinky-white skin.

Harold had taken something from a locker and was polishing it.

'What is that?' I asked him.

'A gun,' he said.

'What for? To shoot frogs?'

He looked a bit embarrassed.

'We don't know whether the natives are friendly.'

'Why should they not be friendly?' I asked, puzzled.

'You never know with natives,' Harold said. 'Do you know the people here?'

'I don't know where we are. But I expect the people are – only people.'

I had been watching something moving, far off over the water against the dazzling sun.

'Look,' I said. 'Here comes one.'

It was a boat. A very small boat. Not much more than a hollowed-out log. And squatting in it was a small boy. His paddle blade made bright splashes in the sun.

'We'll need you as interpreter,' Harold said. But he put the gun aside.

'I will do my level best, sir,' I told him. 'But we have two thousand languages in India.'

'Whoever told you that?'

'Professor Venkatasubramaniam, sir.'

'Oh, well, do your best. Say to the boy: Big White Bird From the Sky comes in peace. And ask him where the nearest white man lives.'

I decided I wouldn't say anything so insulting.

The boy paddled towards us, stopped his little boat, stuck his paddle into the bottom of the floodwater and hung on to it. It showed how shallow this part of the flood was. He held the paddle in the crook of his elbow, made the greeting sign with his two hands, palm to palm, and spoke two words.

'*Nomaskar! Erroplen!*'

I knew the first word was a greeting, but it told me he wasn't speaking my language. And the second word? *Erroplen* – aeroplane. He knew *some* English!

As best I could, I asked him what the nearest town was.

'*Engleesh Gunge.*' He smiled and pointed over the water.

Even Reggie, standing behind me in the hold, got that one.

'But that's where he *said* we'd come down!' I heard him exclaim to Harold. I was amazed at my own fluke. I hadn't really had the right figures to work on. But I wasn't going to admit it. I managed to tell the boy that the aeroplane was broken, and asked him to go for help. He saluted again and paddled off.

'He will go for help,' I told the pilots.

'How long did he say it would take?' Harold asked impatiently.

'I did not ask. Who can tell? This is India.'

I was happy, sitting in the sun in the open door of the hold, watching the graceful white egrets and the brown paddy-birds wading in the shallower water. I was warm! I hadn't felt warm for nearly a year. I could see the tower of the temple we had nearly run into, and I could make out the carvings of Hindu gods. But there seemed to be no sign of life in the temple. In the distance smoke went up from a huddle of huts on a mound. But, after the boy in the boat, nobody came. I didn't care. This was better than facing the music in Calcutta.

But Harold and Reggie sweated and fidgeted all the morning. Reggie started taking the dead radio to pieces, shaking and peering at things like light-bulbs. Harold climbed down on to the floats, examined the struts and joints, tapped with a spanner on one of the floats that seemed to lie deeper in the water. He pulled a long face and called up to Reggie.

'I think we holed the starboard float. And the struts have had a wrench.'

He climbed aboard and saw me sitting there.

'Keeping a good look out?' he asked. 'Would you like to get on top where you can see better?'

He helped me up on top of the wing and I squatted on the warm metal. From there I could see one or two more distant villages and a fringe of jungle. A boat with a big square sail was drifting past in the middle distance. The crew of three or four men were leaning over the side staring in our direction. I waved and shouted to them and they waved cheerily back, but the boat sailed on. I could see where the river channel went now. If we had come down along it we wouldn't have gone aground yesterday. But we'd gone across it, and ended up a long way from the bank.

Another boat was coming down-river. It seemed to be heading towards us, as I stood up and waved again, and someone was waving back, someone in a sun-helmet. I could hear the put-put-put of some sort of engine.

I leant over the wing and called down into the cabin.

'Rescue is approaching, I think, sir!'

It was a long, low river launch and it seemed to be towing a sort of punt. At the nearest stretch of swirling river water it turned upstream into the current, and somebody on board dropped an anchor. Then three men got into the flat-bottom punt and one of them paddled it towards us. There was one plump man in a khaki suit and sun-helmet, one short man with glasses, carrying a bag, and the man with the paddle looked like a local policeman. I got down and stood at the loading-door with Harold and Reggie to greet them. The Englishmen didn't look too happy. I heard Harold mutter to Reggie, and glance aside for his gun.

'Not a white man among them!'

But the cheerful voice that rang out over the water from the plump man was unmistakably speaking English. Indian English, but fluent.

'Good day to you, sirs! I trust you are none the worse for your mishap. I am J. K. Chaudhury, District Postmaster, at your service. I am instructed that you have mail on board, is that not so? No harm has come to the mail, I hope!'

'I'd almost forgotten about the bloody mail-bags,' Harold muttered. He shouted back to the man in the boat, 'Hello! Nice of you to come. Yes, the mail's all right. A pity it's a bit later than we meant.'

The boat was approaching the loading-door.

'We must do our level best to ensure delivery,' said the man in the boat. 'The Royal Mail must get through, eh, what?' And he laughed cheerfully as if he had invented a joke.

'You mean you've come to collect it?' Harold asked, disbelieving.

'I am so instructed by telegraph from Calcutta,' came

the answer. 'I may show you full credentials and give receipt for each bag.'

'Better come on board, then,' Harold said.

The policeman clung to the struts of the float. We let down a metal ladder and the man with glasses clung to the bottom of that. Plump Mr Chaudhury heaved himself up the ladder into the hold. He gave me a funny look as if he hadn't expected to see me there. There was an awkward silence.

'Will you take coffee, sir?' I asked him. I had a feeling this job would take time.

He and the clerk accepted, after twice refusing. And I went to make it in the little galley. It was that rather nasty stuff in a bottle, and the condensed milk came out of a tin, but you had to be hospitable, didn't you? This was India.

When I got back with the coffee-mugs the postmaster was squatting on the floor, chatting, and the clerk was checking the labels on the mail-bags, and writing the details on to buff-coloured forms that rested, with an uncorked bottle of ink, on the top of his battered cardboard suitcase. The policeman was taking the bags as the clerk lowered them out of the door, and was piling them on to the shallow boat, looking anxiously at the waterline.

Then the clerk was saying something excitedly to the postmaster in their language, from the middle of the hold.

'What's the trouble?' Harold asked.

'He says there is irregularity, sir,' the postmaster said. 'One of the bags has been tampered with.' Of course they'd found the one I'd slept in.

Mr Chaudhury got to his feet and had a look.

'Have you any idea, gentlemen, who can have opened this bag?' he asked Harold and Reggie. They both looked at me.

'Did you, by any chance, Murugan?' Reggie asked.

'No, sir,' I said. It was true. Why should I take the blame? Barbara was six thousand miles away, in England.

'Regulations require that in the circumstances full report must be rendered, and I may give you receipt for each item of correspondence remaining in the bag,' said the post-master.

'Oh, my God!' I heard Harold mutter. But the little clerk took out a different form from his suitcase and squatted down to check each crumpled letter which had been my mattress. I knew I was back in India then. Harold and Reggie went off in disgust to the cabin and left them to it.

It was blazing noon by the time the job was done and the policeman had ferried nine boatloads of mail-bags over to the launch on the river.

'We have relieved you of your cargo, Captain,' said Mr Chaudhury to Harold. 'Perhaps you may now float again?'

Harold lowered himself on to the floats once more.

'Just as firmly stuck as ever,' he said. 'Can you send us a floating crane or something?'

'May I suggest an elephant?' said Mr Chaudhury.

Harold glared at him as if he had made a silly joke. But it wasn't a bad idea.

Harold climbed back on board.

'One of us will have to go to Calcutta,' he decided. 'Reggie, we'll toss for it.'

They flipped an English penny and Reggie won.

'What about the boy?' he asked. 'Shouldn't we drop him off in Calcutta too? He lives thereabouts, doesn't he?'

Thereabouts? Only another eight hundred miles away, my home was. And even there I didn't really have a home. They were going to drop me off in a strange, crowded city. *Outer darkness, weeping and gnashing of teeth.*

'Do you not wish me to remain as your interpreter, sir?' I suggested to Harold.

'Okay, if you're not in a hurry,' Harold said. But I could see he was pleased to have company, even mine. 'How long will it be before help arrives?' he asked the postmaster.

'Who can tell?' was the cheerful reply. 'The floods have rendered travel very difficult.'

So off Reggie went with a leather bag, sitting a bit unhappily in the shallow punt. Halfway to the launch he pointed downwards into the water, and called back to Harold.

'Fish! I say, old boy, I left my trout rod in the cabin. Use it, by all means!'

I was just as grateful for that fishing rod as Harold was. Not that he let me use it. And we didn't need fish; we had plenty of tinned sardines and salmon. But it stopped Harold fidgeting. Tell an Englishman to sit and meditate for half an hour, and he'll fidget. But put a fishing rod in his hands and he'll happily do nothing for hours.

He asked me to go back to my look-out on top of the plane, and I didn't mind at all.

The splashing sound of paddles. I looked round. Another boat was approaching the aircraft, a large flat-bottomed one with half a dozen men in it. I called down to Harold.

'Another boat coming, sir!'

'That's quick!' Harold said, thinking of rescue. 'Unless it's only the milkman. Okay, I won't shoot.'

There was one man standing up in the boat, wearing some sort of uniform and a grubby sun-helmet. The paddlers were wearing ordinary Indian dress, not very much at all. They all looked quite young. Once more I began to worry about having to interpret, but once more a voice rang out in Indian English.

'Hello! Customs and Excise!'

'I might have known it,' Harold groaned. 'They've come to count the whisky bottles.' He reeled in his fishing line.

The young man in uniform climbed easily in through the loading-door. It looked quite a long time since he had last shaved, but he had piercing dark eyes.

'Peppahs? Peppahs?' he demanded, making signs with his hands. He seemed to have very little English after all.

'What does he want? Pepper?' Harold asked me.

'Papers,' I interpreted the pronunciation.

'Oh, Lord, I suppose he does,' Harold groaned again. 'Reggie looked after the papers, but I suppose I can find them.' He climbed up the ladder to the cabin. He was followed by the customs officer – if that's what he was. Some of the other men jumped on board. They looked at me hard and one of them asked me a question I didn't understand.

But another one spoke to me in the southern Indian language which I use.

'What are you doing here, boy?' he asked, a bit contemptuously.

'I flew from England in this aeroplane,' I told him haughtily. Then I wished I hadn't said that.

'Passport?' he demanded.

Where was it? Rochester? Bude? I remembered the fuss about passports when we landed from the ship in England. They could put you in prison if you hadn't got a passport.

Suddenly there were shouts and the sound of a scuffle from the flight cabin. Two of the men sprang up the ladder. More grunts and scuffles – then there was Harold being pushed down the ladder by the two men in Indian dress, both of them holding long sharp knives. The man in uniform followed.

'Customs officers?' Harold was shouting. 'You're a bunch of common thieves! You won't get away with this!'

It might have been some misunderstanding, but I didn't think so. Those nasty knives! The postmaster had been real, but these customs men weren't.

I backed away towards the shelf in the hold where I knew Harold had put aside his pistol. Nobody was taking much notice of me. I reached up behind me. The heavy gun was in my hand. I pointed it towards the man in uniform, and my hand shook like a leaf on a tree. I, Murugan, had in my hand a machine that could make a man die!

'Go away!' I managed to say. 'Go away and leave us alone. Or I might kill somebody.'

The men looked quite scared. I think it was because my hand was wobbling so much. The gun could have gone off and hit any one of them.

I heard Harold's quiet voice. 'Well done, young fellow! You tell them.' The long knives were still at his throat, and I couldn't kill them all at once.

The man who spoke my language was nearest to me. He was looking very hard at the pistol in my hand. He took a step towards me. I aimed the gun at him.

'Don't move!' I said. 'I don't want to kill you.' I didn't. He was one of my people.

Watching the gun very carefully, he took another step forwards. Even I couldn't miss him at this distance. I just had to jerk this trigger thing, didn't I? And the bullet would come out and make a hole in him and he wouldn't be alive any more.

'I don't want to kill you,' I repeated. I was almost weeping. He kept coming towards me. I couldn't believe I was going to kill a man. I pulled at the trigger and dreaded the explosion. Nothing happened. He was reaching out for me. I put my left hand to the pistol too, and pulled with all the strength of my fingers. Still nothing happened, and the man took the gun from my exhausted hands.

He turned and said something to the other men.

'Safety catch!'

And they all laughed. They told me afterwards there's a little switch thing on a pistol, and if it's turned on you can't shoot.

Well, then the gun was passed to the leader of the gang, and he turned the safety catch off and pointed it at Harold, and Harold gave up struggling. And he and I were bundled out into the boat, where the men pointed long *spears* at us! And the men set about stripping the plane of everything they could move and find room for in the boat. Enamel mugs and plates, Reggie's sextant, files of papers, tins of food and bits of radio and my discarded winter clothes, they were all chucked into the bottom of the boat. Then they paddled off with us, the boat rather low in the water.

Harold sat gloomily in the stern alongside me.

'I thought you said the natives were friendly,' he said.

'I didn't,' I told him. 'I said the people were people. It seems some of them are bad.'

'Ask them what they are going to do with us,' Harold said. I didn't want to ask, but it was my job as interpreter. I asked the man who spoke my language. He said he didn't know.

'Ask the man in charge,' Harold ordered. I tried again. The question went to the man in uniform and back again through me.

'They say they will consider,' was all I could tell Harold.

But I began to chat quite freely with the man who spoke my language. It was such a joy to use it again! He said his name was Jothi, and, yes, he had travelled eight hundred miles to be with this leader. Were they robbers? No, he smiled. They were Freedom Fighters. I told him my brother called himself a Freedom Fighter and he was in prison. Had he heard of him: Shanmugam from Adyar? Jothi said there were thousands of them in prison, but he thought he had heard of Shanmugam!

'Well?' Harold interrupted. 'What's he saying?'

I thought he was rude to interrupt.

'He says they are not robbers,' I told him.

Harold looked at the loot in the boat and snorted.

'Good of him to say so!' He shrugged his shoulders.

We had paddled carefully round the edges of ricefields, keeping over the irrigation ditches, I suppose, but now we had come to a flooded jungle glade, with thickets of bamboo and broad-leaved trees on each side. The sun made dappled shadows and sparkling reflections on the water. An Indian cuckoo sang from the branches. I felt happy, but I could see that Harold wasn't. I asked Jothi where we were going.

'You will see,' he told me.

We threaded our way between islands of jungle, sometimes with the drowned bushes scraping the underside of the boat. The sun was now this side, now that side. How could anyone remember all the turns? And then we were there!

There's an English fairy story about a princess who went to sleep for a hundred years, and her palace was overgrown with briars and thorns. Well, here was the palace! But I don't suppose it had taken a hundred years. The jungle grows quickly in India. Creepers had crept up the columns of this palace, jungle grass sprouted from its roof, trees had forced their way up through the stones of the court yard, and its walls were splotched with the black slimy mould that spreads in the humid rainy season. Some rajah must have lived here once, but now it seemed deserted except for a troop of monkeys gambolling over the roof. There was a smell of wood smoke hanging about it, though – and wasn't that the smell of spicy Indian food cooking?

The boat bumped against the top of a flight of broad steps, most of which were under the floodwater. We got out.

Harold looked around at the crumbling palace.

'Grand Hotel, eh?' he joked. 'It's what I've been looking forward to.'

The sun went down quickly behind the lush jungle, and it turned black and threatening. A couple of young women in simple green saris brought lamps, little bowls of oil with wicks burning in them, and straw mats for us to sit on. One of the women gave me a motherly smile – or big-sisterly perhaps. She wasn't all that much older than me. Harold was bewildered. Nobody told us where to go or what to do, and the weapons all seemed to have been put away. But the boat had disappeared, too.

The women came back with squares of banana leaf and put them down in front of each of the men, including Harold and myself. Then they came again and ladled out mounds of rice, and richly spiced vegetables. My mouth was watering so much I could hardly wait. Real food, after all those months of grey sliced beef and tasteless cabbage! But Harold looked at his banana leaf with horror.

'What am I supposed to do with this?' he demanded.

I reminded him to eat with the fingers of his right hand only. I did not want the people to think my English friend was impolite.

'They can't treat me like this!' Harold exploded. He was sitting awkwardly on the floor, with his knees up, and scratching furiously at the swelling mosquito-bites on his red legs.

'They treat you like one of the family, sir,' I tried to reassure him. But he was so unhappy that I remembered the stolen enamel plates and the cutlery, and asked Jothi to get the women to bring some for Harold. Of course he was hungry, and though he spluttered and said it was too spicy, he got quite a lot of food down.

When the food was gone Harold turned to me again.

'Well, where's the lock-up? Where are they going to put us for the night?'

I passed the question to Jothi and he told us we could sleep where we liked. The other men were already curling up on the mats on the hard floor. A full moon lit up the verandah of the palace, lighting up the jungle almost as clearly as sunlight.

I heard poor Harold turning on the hard floor and scratching his bites and trying to get comfortable. But I'd had a long day myself and I drifted off into sleep.

I don't know how long I had slept when something woke me up. I opened my eyes. The full moon had shifted but it was still strong. In the shadow at the back of the verandah a large figure was creeping stealthily towards the pile of loot in the corner. The other sleepers did not stir. Harold's place was empty – that must be him moving about. He picked something up from the pile, something shiny. Then he walked out into the moonlight. I could see his shoes tied by their laces round his neck. He was trying to escape!

What should I do? Tell the others? Go with him? Or just keep quiet?

No, I couldn't let him go off into the jungle like this. I knew jungles!

I got to my feet and crept after him on my bare feet.

I saw him go to the edge of the steps and carefully down them, like a bather in England testing the water to see if it was too cold. It wouldn't be cold here, but how deep was it? He moved away from the steps with the water sloshing around just below his waist. All right for him, but it would be up to my chest. I must catch up with him before it got deeper.

I tried to get into the water without splashing. But he spun round. From the thing in his hand came a bright light, directed straight at me. It was the powerful hand-torch from the plane, though he hardly needed it in that moonlight.

He let me catch up with him, wading through the water.

'Go back, Murugan!' he whispered sharply. 'Stay with your people!'

'But, sir!' I whispered back. 'You cannot go through the jungle at night. It is dangerous!'

'I don't mind risking my life. No need to risk yours.'

'You may need my help,' I said.

He turned towards the jungle.

'Come on, then!'

Stumbling on underwater growths we could not see, we reached the moon-shadow of the jungle trees. The moon is strange. Its light seems bright as day, but its shadow is always dark as night. We paused before we plunged into the darkness, and looked back towards the moonlit palace. Was that a white-clad figure, standing on the verandah, staring out over the water?

'Quick!' hissed Harold. 'Take cover!'

He plunged towards a bushy tree whose thick, dark branches dipped down into the water. But I grabbed his arm and tried to hold him back.

'Take care, sir! Take care!'

He stopped in the darkness. At least they couldn't see us from the palace now.

'What's the matter? Have you seen something?'

'No, sir. But please give me torch. We must look with care.'

He gave me the torch. I switched it on, very carefully parted the branches of the leafy tree, and shone the light in.

Twining branches. But, twined along the branches, and from branch to branch like – like that stuff they had put on the tree at Christmas in Bude – something else. I couldn't help drawing in my breath with a hiss.

'I can't see anything,' Harold whispered. Then a little eye reflected the torchlight, and another, and another. And Harold saw.

He jumped back. '*Snakes! Ugh!* Why didn't you tell me there would be snakes?'

'I advised you to take care, sir.'

'No, I'm not a coward,' Harold was muttering to himself. 'I'd even thought of tigers. But not all those snakes.'

'They come from open ground,' I told him. 'And climb trees to get away from the water. Better not to disturb them.'

'You're right. Come on, we're going back.'

We paused at the edge of the jungle shadow and looked back to the verandah. The figure we had seen was not there. No one challenged us as we waded back. What had it been? A broken column in the moonlight? A ghost?

13

Shanmugam

'Good ball!' Harold shouted.

The ball I had bowled hit his off stump. Well, the stump was only a line I had drawn with charcoal on the palace wall, and the pitch was the long tiled terrace. But the cricket bat and ball were good ones, though a bit old. I had found them in an attic of the palace, along with bundles of polo sticks and mouldering saddles. And they gave us something to do in our captivity.

We changed places. I even had a cut-down bat that fitted me. Harold took the ball, ran up to the charcoal mark on the tiles at his end of the pitch, and swung his arm over. The ball hit an interesting bump on the terrace, but I saw it coming just in time and played rather a good defensive stroke. Harold was impressed.

'Who taught you to play cricket, young feller?' he asked.

'Mr Ramaswami,' I told him.

'There was a Ramaswami who played against England in 1936,' Harold said.

'He coached me in Madras,' I said.

'You were coached by a Test cricketer?' Harold exclaimed. 'Then I don't feel so bad about you bowling me out.'

I drove the next ball along the terrace. It was bounding towards the steps and the floodwater. But Jothi, who had been strolling along the terrace, leapt on it, picked it up and slung it back to the bowler in one graceful movement.

'Well fielded!' Harold called, almost too surprised to catch the returned ball. 'Another cricketer! I always said sport holds the Empire together.'

'Tell him not to bet money on it,' Jothi muttered to me in our language. As I thought, he understood more English than he let on.

Jothi girded up his waist-cloth and stood there to field the balls that I hit. I was determined to get one past him, and after a few attempts I did. The ball sped to the edge of the steps and went over.

We all ran after it – we couldn't afford to lose balls in the floods. Jothi waded in bare-footed, and fished it out. The water came just above his knees, and another of the terrace steps was dry in the sun.

'Sir, the floods are going down,' I said to Harold. I thought it might cheer him up.

'I hope they've got Mercury off the mud,' he said gloomily. 'The lower the water, the harder it will be.'

Jothi spoke to me in my language and I translated for Harold.

'Sir, Jothi says the timber firm has sent two elephants.'

But this news did not cheer Harold up either.

'Elephants? Great clumsy things! Look, I *must* be in charge of salvage work. Tell him so.'

I translated back for Jothi. This was my daily job now,

174

go-between for Harold and our captors. I didn't get much thanks from either side for it. They might play cricket together, but they didn't really understand each other. This time Jothi only smiled, then he was called away by one of the other men.

He came back to me that evening.

'We want Mr Harold to write a letter to Government, pleading for action to release him. He must say he is in danger for life and limb.'

'Is he in danger?' I asked.

'As you see, he is well fed and plays cricket. But we wish him to say he is in danger. Tell him we may have to cut off one of his ears and send it to Government.'

I was horrified. Cut off Harold's ear? To think of one of those big red ears being posted to Government in an envelope! And how would they cut it off? Slice it off with a knife, or snip round it with scissors? I couldn't bear to think of it, much less tell Harold about it.

I went to Harold.

'They want you to write a letter, sir. To say how much you are suffering.'

'Suffering?' he snorted. 'Bored to death, I may be. And those damned mosquitoes. But I can put up with it.'

'But, sir, if you do not write the letter you will never get free from here.'

'What do they want?' he asked. 'A ransom? My family's got no money, and Imperial Airways can always find another pilot.'

'I think they want exchange of prisoners, sir. If Government lets one of the Freedom Fighters out of prison, you too will be released.'

'I'm damned if I'll write!' he swore. 'Those terrorists deserve their prison sentences. I've done nothing wrong.'

I looked at his ear, all swollen with mosquito-bites.

Should I tell him? No. A threat like that would make him more pig-headed. It wouldn't work.

I went back to Jothi and told him. He talked to the other men, then came over to me.

'Murugan, you have been to English school. You can write like an Englishman. Write the letter and sign it for him.'

'They will know it is not his handwriting,' I objected.

'That would take time,' said Jothi. 'Do it. Think of thousands of prisoners like your brother. Do you not want one to be freed?'

So I agreed. It wouldn't be the first time I was deceitful. I had sent that false message from the sky over Delhi. They brought me pen and paper looted from the plane, and I squatted down, trying to think how Harold would write a letter. This is how it came out.

From Somewhere in India.

Sir,

I have the honour to submit that I am in the hands of the Freedom Fighters of India in a locality which I have no means of identifying. I beg to request that no steps may be taken by the Armed Forces to procure my release, as such action would certainly result in my demise.

I respectfully inform you that, unless negotiations are expedited for my release in exchange for a prisoner named by Freedom Fighters, loss of one of my ears may ensue. It may be mailed to you via the usual channels.

Though I am naturally willing to lay down my ears for the British Empire, I wish to spare my family the shame and anguish which they would suffer from my mutilation.

I have the honour to be,
   Sir,
   Your obedient servant,
   Harold

And then – panic, I couldn't remember his surname! How could I forge his signature if I didn't know his name? What had that signal from the Viceroy said? *Pilots Thorpe and – Singer*, that was it. I had never seen him write it, but I scribbled it the way Englishmen usually scribble their signatures.

I showed the letter to Jothi and helped him translate it back.

'Is it not a bit cold and stiff, from one who may have his ears cut off?' Jothi objected.

'No, no,' I assured him. 'That is the way the English write.'

I didn't feel too bad about this forgery. It might actually be saving Harold's life – or at least one of his ears.

Next morning I knew – though Harold didn't – that another little boat had slipped away through the flooded jungle, carrying that letter.

Days passed – I lost count of them. The floodwaters fell a little, then rose again. It was still early in the monsoon season, and it could go on for weeks. Unless rain stopped play, Harold and I perfected our cricket strokes daily.

'You'll be able to show them, when the cricket season starts next term at Rochester,' Harold told me.

Rochester? It seemed a long way off. Would I ever get back there? Did I want to? I was happy enough in that old palace, exploring the crumbling rooms, getting fed on delicious food, looking out from the roof over the treetops of the jungle, watching the birds and the monkeys and sometimes a bigger animal – a leopard, maybe.

Then one morning two of the men, the ones I didn't like much, came up to Harold in a hurry. One of them had the pistol, and was pointing it at Harold. They hustled him off to the inside of the palace. There was a room without windows there, a black hole – storeroom, prison cell, torture chamber? I tried to follow.

'What are you going to do to him?' I demanded. One of the men gave a nasty grin and made slicing motions round his own ear.

Oh, no! I felt sick, terrified. I rushed off to find Jothi, someone I could talk to. But he was nowhere to be found.

Then I heard the sound. A distant mutter, a rumble. Thunder? No. Why did it remind me of a chilly classroom with the windows open on wet slate roofs? It *was* that sound, that I had heard first in Rochester. Aeroplane engines warming up. Four 340-horsepower Napier Rapier engines, spluttering into life, somewhere the other side of that jungle.

I ran up the rickety, rotten staircase of the palace. I was in the attics, littered with disjointed furniture, where I'd found the cricket gear. I knew there was a sort of hatchway that led to the roof. I pushed through it and a family of monkeys lolloped quickly away over the roof, babies clinging upside down to their mothers.

I was looking out over the jungle trees, where the shrieking flocks of parakeets flew. It seemed to go on for ever, that jungle, but somewhere on the other side of it must be the open water of the river. And Mercury must be on it, perhaps ready for take-off once those engines reached full power.

Mercury *was* taking off! I knew what that full-pitched roar meant, travelling beyond the trees. And suddenly the jungle wasn't muffling the sound any more. There was the great silvery bird, clear of the treetops, circling to gain height – and heading straight towards me! Now I could even see the two men in it. Surely one of them must be Reggie!

I jumped and capered about on that rooftop like a

madman. And though I knew they couldn't hear me in the plane, I shouted at the top of my voice.

'*Reggie!* It's me, Murugan! They've got Harold down in the dungeon! They're cutting off his ears! You're in the nick of time!'

Neither of the pilots even waved back. The plane banked round, levelled off, and flew away in a straight line. Soon it was only a dot over the distant trees.

And then I saw myself as those pilots must have seen me – if they'd seen me at all. Just another tiny brown ant in the teeming jungle. And a great feeling of desolation came over me. Would I ever be anything more than that, now? One of India's hundreds of millions?

I went slowly down that crumbling staircase. The men were marching Harold along the corridor, the gun still held at his back. I forced myself to look where his ears ought to be. They were both still there.

His cheeks were wet beneath his eyes. He saw me on the staircase and rubbed his face.

'God, it was hot in that black hole! Did you see Mercury? I heard the engines go over, but they wouldn't let me look.'

He wiped his face again, but it wasn't sweat. I was watching an Englishman weep – though it had taken the sound of 1,360 horsepower to make him do it. Harold loved that aeroplane.

They marched him straight to a small boat at the steps, got in with him and another man, and pushed off. It happened so quickly that I was taken by surprise.

'Where are you going? What are you going to do with him?' I called after them. 'Take me with you! The Sahib needs me. Don't leave me behind!'

The men took no notice of me, but I heard Harold's voice.

'Good-bye, Murugan. Thanks for all your help. Look after yourself!'

Look after myself? It seemed I would have to. After they had gone I wandered about the palace, and there was nobody there. Even the women who did the cooking were gone, though they had left the cooking pots and some food.

They'll have to come back, I told myself. *They can't just leave me here in the middle of the jungle.* But couldn't they? I was nobody's business now.

There was a temple attached to the palace. Perhaps they'd gone there? I wandered into it, looking for any sort of human companionship – and found myself face to face with the gods!

Their paint had chipped off, and they had lost some of their many limbs. But I knew who they were. Black-faced Kali scowled at me, with her necklace of human skulls. She was meant to inspire fear, and she frightened me, all alone in the silent temple. But even chubby Ganesha with the elephant head, and prancing Hanuman the monkey god – they didn't look friendly either. Why should these gods seem friendly? I had said they were wicked idols, devils even. And who was this, with six heads and riding on a peacock? I had been told that was Murugan – me! I took myself and my one head quickly out of the temple.

I went back to the deserted terrace. Two cricket bats leant against the charcoal stumps on the wall. Nobody to play with now. And what was the other thing Harold had said as he went? *Thanks for all your help.* What help had I been to him? What help had I been to anybody? To myself, even? I was the loneliest of all India's millions – no friends, no family, nobody to speak to.

I looked out at the jungle. The sun was still quite high, but it was beginning to dip down. I began to hear noises in the palace that I'd never noticed before: shuffles, moans and sighs. Monkeys on the roof? Bats? The wind? *Ghosts?*

Do you believe in ghosts? No? Try sitting all alone in a vast deserted ruin in the middle of the jungle, and ask yourself the same question. There is *something* that hangs around old ruins. And you don't have to wait for darkness.

I wasn't going to wait. I was going to do what I stopped Harold doing – to set off alone into the jungle. It was still daylight. The floods had gone down a bit. Once upon a time there must have been a road to this palace, with ox-carts bringing food for the rajah's feasts, and troops of horsemen cantering down it. *All ghosts now?* But there must be a way out, and I must find it soon.

I went to the place where they cooked the food and found a long slashing knife, the sort that gardeners and foresters use. I tucked some fruit into the cloth which I wore round my waist. That would do. I walked across the terrace and splashed down into the warm water. As I waded out in the direction that the boats went, the water only reached my thighs. But I would have to be careful not to walk into hidden ditches. I kept clear of the snake-infested trees. I remembered where the boats had to wind in and out of the flooded glades, but there was the remains of a straighter track that led up hill and down a bit, and the higher parts were above water. I followed it, and felt that I was getting somewhere. I looked back. The palace had already vanished out of sight. Could I even find my way back if I had to?

I had started off carrying my light sandals, to keep them dry. For the bits of track above the flood level I put my sandals on, for fear of thorns and stinging creatures, scorpions perhaps. But there were just as many thorns under the water – *ouch!*

I hobbled out of the water and looked at the sole of my foot. I remembered the silly old English riddle:

> *I went to the forest and got it,*
> *So I sat me down to look for it,*
> *And because I could not find it*
> *I took it home. What was it?*

But I found the thorn in my foot at last, and managed to pull it out. Then I thought I'd keep my sandals on under the next bit of water, but they got soggy and floppy and were hardly any use at all. Now I wasn't getting anywhere very fast, and I began to worry about the sun sinking down. I had no idea how much daylight I had left. I should have measured the sun's angle and calculated the time to sunset – Reggie's navigating things were all back at the palace. But I hadn't used my brains for weeks.

And I cursed my pampered feet. Once, when I was a poor barefoot child, they used to have thick, horny skin on their soles. But months of wearing school socks and shoes had made them soft. They didn't like this jungle walking – but they'd have to put up with it. There were no wings on my sandals now, no Garuda or peacock to fly on.

I struggled on to the next stretch of water. There was quite a large, circular clearing, with an island of bamboo and other trees in the middle of it, their feathery branches reflected in the calm flood. I suppose it looked quite beautiful in the setting sun, but I had no time to admire it. I was navigating a straight line by that sun, as best I could, because otherwise I might wander through the jungle in circles until I dropped. So I plunged straight ahead into the water and made for the island.

It got quite deep, up to my chest, and then it started getting shallower again. The red sun ahead was alarmingly low. Would I have to spend the night in the jungle? Perhaps this little island wouldn't be a bad place, so long as I had it to myself. But what about snakes?

I came up on to dry ground, among tall jungle grass. I moved carefully, tapping with the flat of my slasher on the ground in front of me. I knew enough about snakes to give them fair warning that I was coming. They usually get out of your way if they can, and only bite you if you tread on them. So I made quite a bit of noise.

Something did move out of my way. But that was no snake, making the tall grass sway like that!

I was aware of a strong smell about that island. *Cat!*

There was a sort of tunnel through the grass, with upright bamboo stems showing at the end of it. Across the end of that tunnel moved a pattern of upright stripes, red, yellow, black. A big animal!

Tiger!

Do you know what petrified means? Yes, turned to stone. It really feels like that. You can't move if you want to. There I was, balanced on one foot in mid-step with my slasher on the ground. I just stayed like that, I don't know how long. Probably the best thing I could do with that tiger around.

When I could move at all I climbed a tree. Maybe that wasn't the best thing to do, but it was what my arms and legs decided. My brain recalled only one useless bit of knowledge: *the Kadamba tree is sacred to the god Murugan*. Was this a Kadamba tree? As I scrambled up the rough branches, I didn't stop to find out.

I stopped when I felt I was so high that a tiger couldn't reach me. I had left my slasher at the bottom. It might have been useful to beat back a climbing tiger, but I wasn't going down again to fetch it.

So there I was, in the crotch of a branch that grew out

over the water, with the red sun dipping down behind the jungle and a Bengal tiger prowling around somewhere beneath me.

My voices, the ones that had spoken when I was in the hold of the aircraft, they started speaking again. Only this time there seemed to be more than two – six, perhaps, one for each of my heads? And there didn't seem to be any answers.

> *Why did you choose such an uncomfortable tree?*
> *Why did you choose an island with a tiger on it?*
> *Is that tiger hungry enough to go off hunting?*
> *Can that tiger swim?*
> *Is that tiger hungry enough to eat YOU?*
> *Can that tiger climb this tree?*
>
> *Why didn't you stay in the old palace?*
> *Why didn't you stay with Reggie and go to Calcutta?*
> *Why didn't you stay at home with Barbara*
> *and William?*
> *Why didn't you stay at school in Rochester?*
> *Why didn't you stay at the mission in Madras?*
> *Why didn't you stay an ordinary Indian boy?*

And so on and so on. The answering part of my brain didn't seem to be there. I tried to stop thinking altogether, just listening to the jungle noises. The sounds of day ceased, and the sounds of night began, the sizzle of night insects and the calls of night prowlers. And – just in case I might have forgotten about him – a short snarling roar. The tiger was still there.

I must just concentrate on staying in that tree. Mustn't drop off to sleep. *Drop off* – it had a very real meaning to me now! If I dropped off I'd be supper for a tiger.

Water noises from the flood. A regular splashing sound.

Was the tiger wading off from the island? No, the sounds seemed to be getting nearer. An even bigger animal, coming my way? Surely not an elephant?

And then – voices! Not inside my head this time, I thought, though how could I be sure? One voice which I knew as well as I knew my own. But it couldn't be, not in the middle of a Bengal jungle.

I tried to look in the direction of the voices, without falling off my branch. There was a pale light gliding over the water. The light seemed to come from a human face, floating silently above the water. And I knew that face too. It was the face of my brother Shanmugam. And I knew what it meant. I had fled the ghosts of the palace to meet the ghosts of the jungle. I was seeing my brother's ghost, and it had come to haunt me for failing to help him.

It is best to speak first, to a ghost.

'Oh, brother,' I gasped out. 'I did my level best to help you!'

That was the most startled ghost I ever expect to see. There was a clatter, the flickering light dropped, and nearly went out. A voice spoke, not Shanmugam's but Jothi's.

'What was that? Don't drop the lantern!'

'I heard my brother speak,' came Shanmugam's voice. 'Are there ghosts in the jungle?'

'Shanmugam!' I called from my tree. 'I'm not the ghost. You are.'

I always argued with my brother, even if he was head of the family.

'Where are you, Murugan?' It was Jothi asking. I had no reason to think that *he* was a ghost.

'Up this tree, Jothi,' I called back.

'Stop playing games, Murugan!' came Shanmugam's voice. 'Get down at once!'

'But there is a tiger!'

'This is no time to play tiger-hunting!' my elder brother said.

I could now see the shape of the boat they were in, drifting directly under my branch. I shifted myself out along it, hung on by my hands as the branch dipped, and dropped into the boat.

I kissed my brother's feet. It's just a thing we do in India, like lifting your hat. They were real feet, not a ghost's.

'Please!' I begged. 'Get away from the island. There truly is a tiger!'

They believed me. With strong paddle strokes, Jothi and Shanmugam drove the boat out into the open water, beneath the stars. It was only then that I saw there was another figure in the back of the boat, his face almost covered with dark hair and beard.

We drifted to a stop again. My brother and I had so much to say to each other. He shone the lantern on me.

'You have grown. But I thought you were at school.'

'I thought you were in jail.'

'I was. They have only just released me.'

'I am glad. Do you know why they released you?'

'No. But they said the order came from the very highest level.'

'That was me, then. I went over the head of the Viceroy.'

'Indeed you cannot get much higher than that. But what do you mean?'

'We flew over his palace in the aeroplane. And I tricked the Englishman into sending a message in Hindi: *release Shanmugam!*'

'You did well, young brother. Perhaps that is why they chose me to exchange for the pilot.'

'I am glad that Harold is released too, he is my friend. I wrote the letter that led to your exchange.'

'Then you did very well, young brother. The pilot will be grateful and will fly you back to England as a reward.'

'Must I go back to England?'

'Of course. You must complete your education. You will become a great man in India. The *guru* here sees it in your stars, do you not, master?'

He spoke these last words to the silent figure in the back of the boat. And, under the stars, the *guru* spoke.

'There will be a great war, in every part of the world. Weapons of destruction will be used such as we do not yet dream of. By the end of seven long years our western rulers will be so weary that they will lose the desire to rule us. They will go home. India will be ruled by Indians. We shall need young men of great skill, knowledge and wisdom.'

'There you are, Murugan. What do you want to be? Pilot of an airliner? Or Prime Minister of India?' my brother asked me.

'Do not mock and laugh at me, Shanmugam,' I begged. 'I have had enough of that.'

The *guru* spoke again.

'We do not mock. One day there will be an Indian who is both these things.'

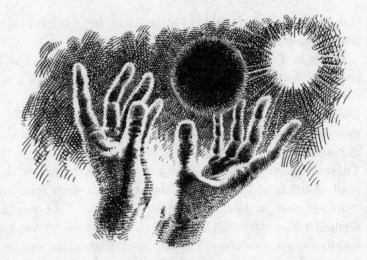

14

Green and Pleasant

Summer in England!

Oh yes, they had flown me back. They had to. Poor Mercury was still too bent to fly home – the elephants had been a bit rough with it. So they put me on one of their big flying-boats, comfortable but boring. It took five days, with stops. No dangerous flying over deserts.

The Easter term was over by the time I got back, so they sent me down to Bude for another cold and boring holiday. I tried to explain to them down there about my urgent family affairs in India, but they couldn't understand why I ran away from school. They said I was forgiven, and I promised not to do it again, and they persuaded the Headmaster to let me go back to Rochester when the summer term began.

There was one thing I had been looking forward to – seeing Mouse again and exchanging stories. What had happened to him and Barbara after I left? But he wasn't at school any more. Hodgkins was there, but he didn't understand my adventure either. He said the Woods family had left Rochester.

Anyhow I was *gated* for the whole term. It meant I couldn't go out at weekends or any other time, not even for a Sunday walk. Shanmugam was free, Harold was free, but I was back in prison. The other boys treated me more like a convict or a lunatic than a hero. Never mind, I did what my brother told me. I got on with my education. There was even a new maths master, Mr Chew, who really liked mathematics.

I had heard a lot about the English spring, but it never seemed to come that year. Instead of shivering on icy football fields we shivered on icy cricket grounds. Because I was no good at football they put me in the most junior cricket game, and I was so frozen that I couldn't play cricket either. But I got myself a job as scorer for junior matches. I enjoyed keeping a neat score-book and working out averages, and it made me quite popular, because I could always tell a boy when he had broken some school record. I needed something to make me popular.

But today, here I was, sitting in a comfortable motor-coach, with sunlight and shadow flickering over the open roof. And the air was *warm* – I couldn't believe it! We had missed spring, but summer had come with a rush. So this was England's green and pleasant land! Trees weighed down with green leaves, cows standing in green meadows, fields of green corn. Even the village duckponds were covered with green duckweed.

Good old Stodge was sitting beside me. He was the wicket-keeper of this 'Colts' team, the under-fifteens. Of course I was only the scorer. But they needed the best players and the best scorer for this away match. The fixture against Framlingham was a very serious affair. We had to win.

'I wonder if Mouse will be playing,' Hodgkins suddenly said.

'What do you mean?' I asked. I couldn't think why he was talking about Mouse.

'He's not very good at cricket,' said Stodge.

'He can't play if he's not with us,' I pointed out.

'I told you he was at Framlingham, didn't I?' Hodgkins said. Had he? Anyway, that was another sunny thought. I might be seeing Mouse today!

We drove through an old town, crowded with traffic and people on foot. The slow-moving coach felt even hotter.

'Please, sir, may we take our blazers off?' I heard Beasley ask.

'Oh, very well. But keep your ties on,' said Mr Percival. He was in charge of the team, and umpire.

'What are we stopping for?' I asked Hodgkins.

'Can't you see the Belisha Beacon?' he said. Oh yes, that was the orange ball on the black-and-white pole. It meant the traffic had to stop to let people cross, didn't it? I wasn't used to English streets.

I watched the ordinary English people going across, men, women, children, prams. Then I suddenly grabbed Hodgkins' arm.

'Look!' I said.

The man crossing the road had a yellow straw hat, a light summer suit and a walking stick. But there was something about the way he walked –

'What's the matter?' Hodgkins asked.

'Where are we?' I said.

He said, 'Ipswich.'

I was being ridiculous. It was because I was shut up in school for so long. I was seeing things. What would my *gentleman* be doing in a place called Ipswich?

We drove on to Framlingham, a school plonked down in the middle of the countryside instead of the middle of a city, but somehow like our own school. As we drove up to it, big Beasley was standing up at the front of the coach and fooling around.

'Look out, Framlingham, here we come!' he called out. 'First person out scores a century!'

The coach stopped. Beasley opened the door and leapt out from the top of the steps.

'*Ouch!*' said Beasley as he landed. He hopped on one foot.

Mr Percival hurried down the coach.

'Beasley, you stupid boy, what have you done?'

'Twisted my ankle a bit, sir. It's nothing. *Ouch! Ouch!*'

Mr Percival and one of the Framlingham masters helped him hobble off to the school sanatorium. The rest of us went to the dining-hall for an early lunch. We filed in and sat on benches down one side of a long table. The Framlingham team filed in the other side. There was someone with fair sticking-up hair grinning and waving.

'Hello, Stodge! Hello, Mugwumps!' Mouse called.

Hodgkins called back, 'How did *you* get on the team, Mouse?'

But then a master called for silence, and for a blessing on the ham, cold potatoes, beetroot and lettuce. We had started eating when Mr Percival came back without Beasley, looking hot and bothered. He called Armitage, our team captain, away from the table. But I could hear what they were saying.

'That silly boy's got a bad sprain. He can't possibly play.'

'Oh, sir, we must field a full team against Framlingham!'

'Then Murugan will have to play instead of scoring.'

'But he's a *weed*, sir! He's no good at anything.'

'Never mind. Find him some kit.'

Armitage made the best of it, putting on a smile as he came back to the Framlingham captain at the table.

'I've got bad news for you, Spencer. You'll be up against our Oriental Wizard. He's better than Ranjitsinhji.'

They all looked at me. The Framlingham boys looked impressed, except for Mouse. Ranjitsinhji was the one Indian cricketer that everyone had heard of, and even the English said he was the best player of his time. But our team were hiding smiles and giggles.

Beasley came hobbling back with a big bandage round his ankle.

'Tough luck, Beezer!' said Armitage.

'Do you think you can manage the scoring, Beasley?' Mr Percival asked him.

'Of course, any fool can score,' Beasley answered rudely. Mr Percival pretended not to hear. But I was worried about Beasley messing up my neat score-book.

There was more laughter in the changing-room when they tried to put me into big Beasley's shirt and white trousers and boots. But Mouse came to my rescue and brought me some clothes and boots that fitted.

'You can borrow my bat, Mugwumps. Promise not to score any runs!'

We still didn't have a chance to talk, not in that crowded changing-room. Framlingham won the toss and went in to bat –

But look, perhaps you don't know about cricket. Some people don't. I think I learnt cricket language before I learnt any other kind of English, but I won't bother you with it.

They told me to stand on the edge of the field and stop the balls rolling off it. You see, if the ball goes off the field the other side scores four points. Actually they put me there to keep me out of the way, as they did on the football field. Never mind, I was happy, standing there in the sun. I could see Beasley sweating away in the scorer's hut, and I was quite sorry for him.

He was busy enough, because Framlingham was scoring a lot of runs. I wasn't busy, because our other fielders stopped the balls before they came my way. They didn't trust me. I tried not to let my mind wander.

Here was one! It came bounding over the green turf towards me, another fielder in hot pursuit. All I had to do was stop it and throw it back to Stodge in the middle of the field. I stopped it.

'Chuck it to me, chuck it to me!' said the other fielder. But I threw it far over his head for Stodge to catch. You don't have to be big to throw far. If Stodge hadn't been so surprised he could have got the Framlingham batsman out.

'Well fielded, Mugwumps!' a high clear voice called from the crowd behind my back. I *knew* that voice. I turned round to look.

There was a group of girls in summery school uniform and straw hats. One of them was waving to me. It was Barbara! I waved back. What was she doing here?

What was that? – another ball, speeding past me along the ground, with the other fielder racing after it. It went off the edge of the field. Four points to the other side.

'You weren't even *watching!*' panted the other fielder angrily. I had heard those words on the football field. I had been looking at a flying-boat that time.

The captain moved me to another part of the field where I had even less to do. I tried to keep my eyes off Barbara. Perhaps I could speak to her at tea-time.

Yes, I suppose cricket's the only game that stops half-

way for tea. We all trooped off the field to the pavilion. A
good cup of Indian tea. And something special, too. What
were those red fruits in bowls? I asked Hodgkins.

'Haven't you met a strawberry before, Mugwumps?' he
asked.

I tasted one.

'They are almost as delicious as mangoes,' I said.

Someone spluttered with laughter behind me. It was
Mouse coming up to us, and choking on a strawberry.

'*Mangoes?* They put them in pickles. They're disgusting!'

'Hello, Mouse,' I said. 'Is Barbara coming for strawberries?'

'Not likely. She's only a visitor.'

Beasley and Armitage were standing together. Beasley
pointed to the crowd.

'Skirts! Pity we can't go and pick them up, eh?'

It was Barbara's little group. I walked over to them
with my strawberry bowl.

'Hello, Barbara. It is nice to see you. Would you like a
strawberry?'

'There!' said Barbara, turning to her friends. 'I told you
he was kind, as well as handsome and clever.'

What *had* she been telling them about me?

I shook hands with Barbara and her four friends, and
we shared out the strawberries. There were not many for
each of us, but that wasn't the only reason why I wished
she was alone. I asked her what she was doing here.

'Haven't you heard? They put me in prison – boarding
school. I'm at St Felix, it's not far from here. They let us
out to watch cricket because it's *good* for us.'

I looked at their freshly ironed green dresses and their
laughing faces.

'I think it is not a bad prison,' I said. 'I would not mind
going there.'

They giggled.

'Ooo, yes!' said a girl with dark curly hair. 'We'll smuggle you in – in a mail-bag.'

Mouse had followed me over. Rather shamefaced, he offered round three strawberries, all he had left.

'Mouse, I've come all the way to *see* you,' Barbara said. 'Aren't you going to bat?'

'Probably not.' He shrugged his shoulders.

'Well, how do you like Framlingham?' his sister went on. He shrugged again. 'All right. I hate being a new boy.' He didn't seem very happy.

And then a bell rang for the game to start again. I took my bowl back to the pavilion.

'You're in last, Murugan,' the captain snapped at me. 'But you're expected to stay with the team, not go off chasing skirts.'

Of course he was only jealous.

Framlingham had declared and it was our innings – sorry, cricket language again! It meant I could sit in a deck-chair in the sun until it was my turn to go and bat. It also meant that we weren't doing very well and we might lose the match. I didn't mind waiting. Cricket's the only game that isn't in a hurry. That's why we like it so much in India. And I didn't much mind if we lost – though of course I wouldn't dare say so. I was happy enough sitting there and knowing that Barbara was at the same ground, and that we might have a few words after the match. I was only a bit worried about my friend Mouse. It was strange to think that an English boy could feel just as lost as I did in a new school. I wished I could help him.

Actually I didn't have to sit for very long – and this also meant that we were losing. I strapped the white pads round my legs, and put the knobbly brown gloves on my hands. I picked up Mouse's bat. It was a good one.

Armitage, the captain, looked down at me.

'We haven't a chance of winning, do you understand? If we can keep going for another twenty-five minutes, it'll be a draw. Keep that bat between the bowler and the stumps. Keep your legs out of the way. And don't try to hit anything. Got it?'

I nodded. What he was telling me to do was impossible. But you don't argue with your captain. I walked out to the middle of the field.

Of course you know that in cricket there are two batsmen at once, one at each end. The other one was Hodgkins. Not many balls got past him, whether he was behind the stumps or in front of them. But he looked worried as he came a little way to meet me.

'I'll try and keep most of the bowling to myself,' he said. 'Don't get hurt, Mugwumps. It's quite fast.'

As I walked to my end of the pitch I heard their bowler mutter to another member of their team.

'Their Oriental Wizard! I'll see if he likes a bit of bodyline.'

I don't know whether he meant me to hear, or didn't think I would understand if I did hear. I knew what he meant. Bodyline meant hurling the ball at the batsman's body or head. It wasn't supposed to happen at nice schools but – you know, sometimes it did.

I looked round the field, with the fielders scattered over it. That was Mouse, standing almost exactly where I had been put. That showed what his team thought of him. He'd been put there to keep him out of the way. I thought perhaps I'd be kind, and hit the ball towards him sometimes to give him something to do. But I wasn't too happy myself. I'd really had no practice since those days at the old palace in the jungle. But still, the sun was shining and I had nothing to lose.

Three times the bowler sent the ball down the pitch to me, and three times I stopped it hitting the stumps behind me. Then it was Stodge's turn the other end and he did the same thing six times. It wasn't very exciting. No wonder some people think cricket is a dull game. I saw some of the spectators packing up and going away. I hoped Barbara would stay.

My turn again to face the fast bowler. He took a long run, leapt into the air, swung his arm over and let the ball go. It hit the ground, bounced up and hit me on the cheek bone.

I lost my balance, toppled over, and lay on the ground. I could see the ball speeding off the field behind me.

Everyone was terribly worried. The Framlingham team clustered round me, and I saw Mouse racing up from the deep field to see how I was. Mr Percival trotted up in his white umpire's coat. Stodge ran from the other end of the pitch and helped me up.

The fast bowler said, 'Awfully sorry, old chap! It must have hit a bump.'

I picked up the bat, stood in front of the stumps again, and said I was all right. Everybody clapped. I was a brave little hero. Actually it had been a glancing blow and hadn't even hurt much. The game went on.

But it had made me angry. Not with that fast bowler – that was what he wanted, to get me rattled. I was angry with that nasty little red ball that had stung my cheek. It was a wasp, a hornet, a plaguy rat, a vicious snake, and I was going to punish it. My bat was my slashing knife, my war club, my two-handed sword – but still I knew it was a cricket bat and I would use it as Mr Ramaswami had trained me. I had forgotten my captain's orders: *Don't try to hit anything.*

I forgot whether we were winning or losing. I kept my

eye on that hard little ball and *hit* it. Sometimes I killed it dead in front of me, but more often I drove it off into the open spaces of the field. When it started coming at my head again I ducked and swatted it as it went by. I even ran half-way towards it and beat it before it leapt at me. I kept hearing Stodge calling to me, '*Run*, then!' and we ran. But I'd almost forgotten about running.

If there were claps and cheers from the crowd now I didn't notice them. But at last I noticed a silence – a sort of *deathly hush*. Had everybody gone home? For the first time I looked round at the crowd. They were still there, and I could feel all their eyes on me. And I looked at the scoreboard and saw what the figures meant. We could *win* this match!

Only three runs needed to win! I could be the hero of the school. Flying to India and back was nothing – this was something they could understand. And I could do it at one stroke. I screwed myself up for that last effort, every muscle tense.

The ball came at me, and I lashed out at it with all my strength. It soared up into the air, and I could hear my team cheering the winning hit from the pavilion.

There was only one fielder anywhere near that ball. He was running desperately towards it, hands lifted to catch it. It was Mouse.

The ball fell into Mouse's hands and he held on to it.

Wild cheers filled the air. The school had its hero. But the school was Framlingham and the hero was William Woods. The game was over. They had won and we had lost.

But they clapped me too as we all walked back to the pavilion. Mouse ran up to me. I held out his bat to him, but he gripped me by the hand.

'Oh, I'm *sorry*, Mugwumps! But thanks for the chance!'

You know, I think he needed to be a hero more than I did.

And then there were female arms hugging me and blond hair in my eyes and a kiss – *ouch!* – right on my bruised cheek.

'Well *done*, Mugwumps!' came Barbara's breathless voice.

'But I lost the match,' I told her.

'Who cares? It was *fun*, watching you. When can we see you again?'

'I don't know. Where's St Felix?'

'Not far from Daddy's job. It's very hush-hush. At Felixstowe.'

'Where's that?'

'Oh, you're hopeless! Near Ipswich.'

A schoolmistressy voice called, 'Barbara! *Barbara!*'

'Coming, Miss Blewitt!' Barbara called back, and turned away. 'Come and stay with us in the holidays!' she said over her shoulder as she ran off.

The coach trip back to Rochester was rather a silent one. I checked the score-book to see what sort of a mess Beasley had made of it. Where were the four points we should have scored when the ball went off the field from my cheekbone? They weren't there. I suppose everyone had been too interested in my dead body. So it meant we had won after all.

But I said nothing. That's life, isn't it? You think you've lost, and really you've won.

And the evening we got back to Rochester the world went black.

It was just before lights out time in the dormitory. The windows were wide open to the stuffy summer night, and through them came the sound of great wailing sirens. Then the lights went out. All of them: the lights in The Vines, the lights in all the houses, the lamps in the streets. There was no reflection in the sky from the lights of Rochester, Chatham or Gillingham, all the Medway Towns. We all hung out of the dormitory windows looking at – nothing. *Blackout!*

Rrrrmmmm, rrrrmmmm, rrrrmmmm . . . the propellers of a lone aeroplane were grinding their way across the top of the night.

'Do you think it's a German?' a young voice said excitedly.

'Don't be daft,' said someone else scornfully. 'It's only a practice.'

'You never know, though.'

Then we all gasped as a great column of light leapt from the ground and lit up the high clouds.

'Searchlight!'

Then another shaft of light, and another and another. They swayed and groped about the sky, searching for the sound of that lone aeroplane.

'Got him!'

Like a silvery moth just below the clouds, the lone aeroplane had blundered into the spider's web of searchlights. They all swept towards it and fastened on it, until it glowed brightly in the concentrated beams.

'What about the anti-aircraft guns?'

'Ack–Ack, open fire. Boom! Boom!'

But the searchlights passed the aeroplane from finger to finger, northwards to the Thames estuary, onwards up England's east coast to –

To Ipswich? To Felixstowe?

Barbara's father was doing a hush-hush job in Felixstowe. Perhaps that person I saw in Ipswich might, after all . . .

But even if he was my *gentleman*, what should I do

about it? Give him away again? Or thank him? If it hadn't been for him, I would never have flown to India.

The searchlight went out. There was only darkness, and voices in the dark.

'They say the next war will be the end of civilization as we know it.'

'I hope it goes on long enough for me to join up.'

Someone flashed a hand torch out of the window. A stern voice came from The Vines, *'Put that light out!'* Was that what war was like? Darkness, and you couldn't even shine your own little light?

The night wind blew a gap in the clouds and I could see the stars. I remembered another voice in the dark.

'A great war in every part of the world . . . seven long years . . . they will be weary . . .'

The sirens sang steadily for the all-clear. The lights came on. We went to bed.

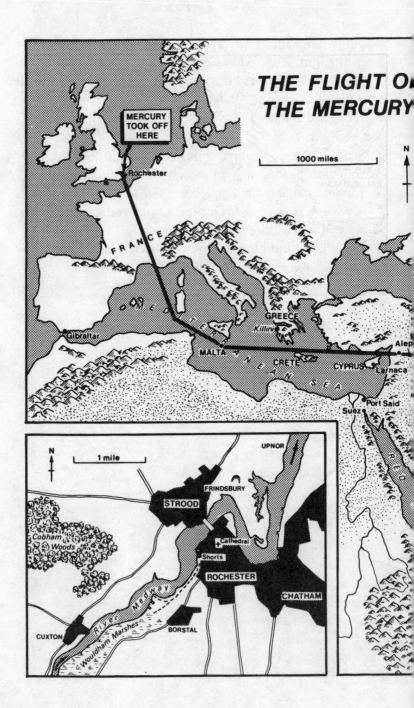

THE FLIGHT OF
THE MERCURY

N

1000 miles

MERCURY
TOOK OFF
HERE

Rochester

FRANCE

Gibraltar

GREECE

Killini

MALTA

CRETE

CYPRUS

Alep

Larnaca

Port Said

Suez

N

1 mile

UPNOR

FRINDSBURY

STROOD

Cobham
Woods

Cathedral

Shorts

ROCHESTER

CHATHAM

River Medway

CUXTON

Wouldham Marshes

BORSTAL

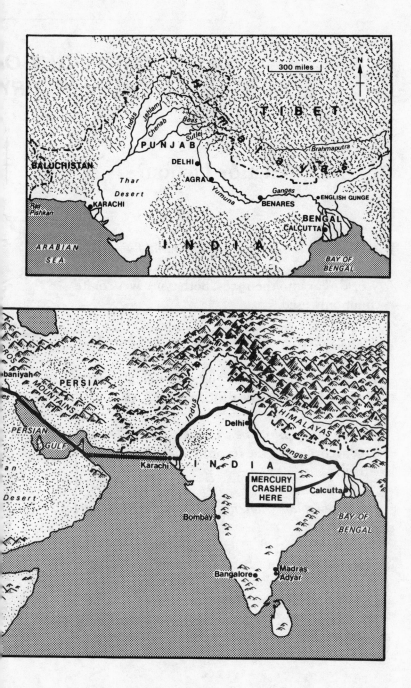

·Fact or Fiction?·

Were there such things as seaplanes and flying-boats?
Yes. For nearly half a century, from before the First World War into the 1950s, both types were quite commonly used.

But was there ever such a thing as the Short Mayo Composite Aircraft?
Yes. As a schoolboy, the author watched some of its trial flights from the River Medway in 1938.

Did the mishaps on the trial flights actually happen?
Yes, according to the record books – or something like them.

Did the seaplane Mercury fly from the Medway to eastern India?
No. But Mercury flew 6,045 miles nonstop from Dundee in Scotland to South Africa, in 42 hours.

Did Mercury make a dangerous forced landing?
No. But some of the Short flying-boats had similar adventures.

Fact or Fiction?

Are the characters in the book real people?
The author has used real names for people he did not know, and invented names for people he did know. But he has tried to tell a story, not to describe any actual persons.

Did the boys at Rochester ask for it?
Yes. But it's a very different school now.